"Come with me, Tracy. I need to hold you in my arms."

Adam held out his hand to her. "Tracy," he murmured as the smooth beat of a gentle love song filled the air.

"Adam, I can't," she whispered.

"Yes, darling, you can. The music's slow, and I'll be with you."

Tracy looked up into his eyes, wanting to take his hand, but afraid.

Suddenly, completely trusting, she did as he asked. He led her through the crowd to the dance floor; once there, he waited a moment while she gathered her courage, then opened his arms. With a soft sigh of relief she stepped into them.

It was awkward at first, but soon Tracy moved closer, until she was nestled in Adam's arms. Neither knew that the band played the song twice, nor that those around them watched in silent pleasure.

As the final notes of the song faded away, they wandered arm in arm through the nearby trees and stopped by a brook that sparkled in the moonlight. Adam drew her close to him, and his fingers tilted her head so he could look into her eyes. As though in slow motion, he bent to kiss her, parting her lips in the caress of a lover. Tracy met his need with the fire he had kindled, and gave herself up to enchantment . . .

WHAT ARE *LOVESWEPT* ROMANCES?

They are stories of true romance and touching emotion. We believe those two very important ingredients are constants in our highly sensual and very believable stories in the *LOVESWEPT* line. Our goal is to give you, the reader, stories of consistently high quality that may sometimes make you laugh, sometimes make you cry, but are always fresh and creative and contain many delightful surprises within their pages.

Most romance fans read an enormous number of books. Those they truly love, they keep. Others may be traded with friends and soon forgotten. We hope that each *LOVESWEPT* romance will be a treasure—a "keeper." We will always try to publish

LOVE STORIES YOU'LL NEVER FORGET
BY AUTHORS YOU'LL ALWAYS REMEMBER

The Editors

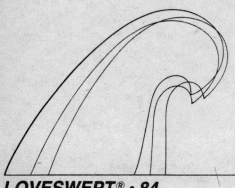

LOVESWEPT® • 84

BJ James
A Stranger Called Adam

BANTAM BOOKS
TORONTO • NEW YORK • LONDON • SYDNEY • AUCKLAND

A STRANGER CALLED ADAM

A Bantam Book / March 1985

ISBN 0-553-21693-7

Published simultaneously in the United States and Canada

For Kathy,
who believes a friend is for keeps

One

"Lost!"

"A child is lost."

"Where?"

"On Shadow."

"Oh, God!"

"Will she come?"

"She must. She and her devil dog."

Like wildfire on a dry summer morning the whispered words spread. Fearful eyes turned, one after another, to the towering monolith whose peak pierced the clouds. Like a miscalculation of God it rose boldly, an angry spear, far above the other softly rounded and tree-strewn mountains. Its roughhewn face hid zigzagging paths that lost themselves in deep, secret caves and mysterious swamps. There were no fields of grassy clover scattered over ridges like a broken necklace of bright green pearls. The dense evergreens that clung tenaciously, their insidious roots penetrating and cracking the unwelcoming granite, grew twisted and gnarled. Stunted and black green, they were as ugly as their hostile host.

In dark reminder and true to its name, as the morning sun rose in the sky, it cast its shadow over the village and the valley that nestled at its base. Then time moved slowly and sound was hushed. Birds ceased their singing; the buzz of insects dwindled. The early rising mountain folk slowed their pace, taking stock of the day, until the sun won free and bathed them in unfettered brilliance.

The people who inhabited the valley of Shadow were compelled to spend a part of each day in a passionate love-hate tryst with the monster that hovered over their rooftops. Yet, beneath it all, they were fiercely proud that this was their mountain.

As with all misfits, the mountain drew the thrill-seekers and the curious. Legends were rife. Not one villager was without his tale of the dark mountain. Many were myth; many were fact.

Adam Grayson had come with pen and camera to record the mountain and its legends. It was his daughter who was lost. She was tiny, and blond, just six years old, and her name was Summer.

"How in the hell could you be so irresponsible?" Adam Grayson whirled in his pacing and stared with piercing eyes at the cowering young teenager. His chest rose and fell in angry agitation, and the hand he raked through his disheveled silver hair was unsteady. "You were to do only one thing—watch Summer."

"But I wasn't gone very long. Summer wanted a drink of water and I went inside to get it. It truly took only a minute, Mr. Grayson." The trembling girl stared down at her hands that were endlessly twisting and knotting a lacy white handkerchief. Her southern drawl dropped to an even softer murmur as she repeated, "It was only for a minute."

"Do you expect me to believe that? Am I suppose to think that in the length of time it took you to pour a glass of water, a six-year-old child could vanish?" Several times his hands opened then clenched into tight, impotent fists.

"It's true, it's true. I swear it." Tears that had gathered in her eyes spilled down her pale cheeks as her painfully thin shoulders shook with heaving, strangling sobs. "She was alone hardly any time at all. I just—Oh, no!"

"What is it?" In the agonized silence her stricken eyes met Adam Grayson's clear gray ones.

"The phone did ring. It was your sister. She asked how Summer was and I said fine. And all the time she was . . . sh-she . . ." A mournful wail, desperately stifled, cut off her words. The knuckles twisting in and out of the mutilated handkerchief were white with strain.

There was a perceptible relenting of Adam's stiff posture, as he sat down and drew the sobbing girl into his arms. He soothed her with gentle hands and crooned words of assurance to her, though his own face was the bleak, wintry hue of despair.

"Shh. Hush, Melinda. I know you didn't mean this to happen. Shh, don't cry. I'm sorry I attacked you. It was only because I was so worried. Hush now, hush. We'll find her." It was a comforting litany for the girl where there could be none for the man. He held her, offering silent apology for his harsh words. He knew in his heart that Melinda was no more to blame than he.

At the first ring of the telephone he was on his feet, snatching the receiver from its cradle. The sharp bark that was both greeting and demand came from an aching, constricted throat.

"Yes?"

"Chief Halloran here, Mr. Grayson."

"Have you found her?"

"No, sir, but we think we might know where she is."

"Then for God's sake, man, tell me so I can go get her."

"It's not that simple, Mr. Grayson." Something about the terse sentence triggered an even greater alarm in Adam. In a cold wave of bitter premonition he fearfully clutched the receiver like a life line and waited for the inevitable. "We think she's wandered on the mountain," Halloran said.

"Shadow?"

"Yes, sir." There was a long pause, then he added inadequately, "I'm sorry."

"What do we do?" The bitter taste of his own blood filled Adam's mouth as he bit down hard on his lip. He struggled to remain calm, fighting the surge of paralyzing fear that could swiftly become unthinking panic.

"I've already called the search teams. They're gathering supplies and equipment. We should be ready to move within the hour, and we've sent a message to Tracy Walker. If anyone can find your daughter, it will be Tracy and Wolfe."

"Tracy Walker?" Even in Adam's dazed mind the name stirred a memory that nearly surfaced, then skittered away to be buried under an avalanche of anxiety and worry.

"Tracy and Wolfe know that mountain like nobody else. I doubt there's a path or a stream they haven't explored over the years."

"Where is he? How long will it take him to get here?"

"Her."

"What?" Again a memory nagged at the raw edges of his mind, nebulous and unformed, but there all the same.

"Tracy Walker is a woman, and Wolfe is her dog. Together they're the best damn trackers in the country. If there's anything lucky about this situation, it's that we have them."

"How long before they get here?" Adam repeated.

"Can't say for sure. Jack Peters has gone over to her cabin at the far side of the valley now. Depends on whether or not she's there and how long he has to wait for her."

"What do we do in the meantime? We can't just stand around. Damn it, man, my daughter's up on that monster." A note of hysteria, foreign to his nature, had begun to creep into his voice.

"We'll be gathering at the base of the mountain at ten-thirty, about an hour from now. That gives the search parties over eight full hours of daylight." Halloran paused, searching for words of comfort, but there were few. "We'll do our best to find her."

"I know you will." Adam's shoulders slumped wearily. His last words had been an apology of sorts for his curtness, but they went unheard. The buzzing of an empty line signaled that Halloran had hung up. Adam stared out the window at the brooding spire of the mountain, hearing in his mind the trill of his daughter's delightful laughter. The very real sound of a smothered sob drew him back from the haunted land of his thoughts.

Replacing the receiver, he turned to the dejected girl who was huddled on the sofa. She was really no more than a child herself. Perhaps the care of a six-year-old had been too much for the teenager. But she and her mother had been so sure, and it had been for only two days.

"Melinda," he said with a return of his characteristic gentleness, "why don't you go on home now? There's nothing more you can do here."

"Oh, no. Please let me stay. I have to know that Summer's been found. That she's all right."

"No, go home. The word's sure to be out, and your mother will be worried. I'll let you know as soon as we have her back." He injected a confidence he did not feel. Now that his initial blind rage had calmed, he knew he had been unfair to heap the blame on her frail shoulders. "Go along now, your mother will be frantic."

"Yes, sir." She rose fluidly, with a hint of the grace that would be hers in the future. At the open doorway she stopped and turned back. "I forgot! I forgot to tell you what your sister said. She's all through with her doctor's appointment and she'll be here tomorrow."

"Thank you, Melinda." He turned unseeing eyes away from the waiting girl. When he said no more she quietly opened the screen door and stepped onto the porch.

"Damn!" The word exploded from Adam as he

slammed his hand against the wall. The irony of it was too much. "Why couldn't you have come today, Liza? Then Summer wouldn't be lost and wandering on a great, hulking mountain."

"I think it's safe to assume that she's still on the lower side. There's no way she could be too far up; it's just been a bit over two hours." Chief Halloran was standing in the middle of a group of men, each dressed in heavy clothing and boots to withstand the vicious brambles and vines of the dense undergrowth they would be searching through. "If it weren't for these damn caves and the swamp, we could probably find her easily."

"I don't think she would go into a cave," a deep voice called.

"And I wouldn't have thought she would go up the mountain," Halloran snapped, and fixed the protestor with a stern stare. "We will check the caves."

The murmur of the gathering crowd rose and fell, a pulsating sea of sound. First one grew quiet and then another, until total silence preceded the tall silver-haired man who made his way to the group around Halloran.

"If she's in those caves we'll never—" The speaker stopped, saying no more when he realized that it was Adam Grayson who stood at his side.

"What about the caves?" Adam said quietly.

Halloran flicked a concerned look at the composed face before him. Such calm was unnatural. He had enough to worry about with the little girl. If the father lost control, he'd have his hands full. A keen assessment of the pale gray eyes showed no lurking hysteria. Matching stare for stare, each took the measure of the other.

They were of a size, and in a fractional flicker of recognition each understood that they were of a kind. Halloran realized that Adam Graywon would approach a given situation much as he himself would, coolly and controlled, with shattered emotions masked. He decided to be brutally truthful, to give Adam the unvarnished facts. It was what he would prefer.

"What about the caves?" Adam prompted when he saw Halloran's decision had been made.

"This side of the mountain is riddled with honeycomb caverns. Some have been explored and charted, some haven't. There are some that go deep into the heart of the mountain." Their eyes met, Halloran's holding a warning.

"And Summer could be lost in one of the caverns?" At Halloran's nod Adam closed his eyes for a second, hiding the resurgent fear in them. Shaking it aside, he asked the question that had to be asked. "Are they large enough that she could lose her way and not be able to find the entrance?"

"Some of them." Halloran put no softening frills on the truth. He knew Adam would not need them.

"Then we'll be lucky to find her." Summer's place in his heart was a raw, ragged ache.

"You've forgotten, Mr. Grayson. We have something on our side. We have Tracy. She knows those caves, and Wolfe can find your daughter's trail when no other dog could." Halloran's hand on Adam's shoulder was kind, offering what little encouragement he could.

"Jed, could I speak to you a minute?" The small spare man had just joined the group. He drew the chief out of earshot and spoke animatedly, gesturing wildly. Jed Halloran shook his head sadly, his gaze never leaving Adam's face as he listened. Then with slow, reluctant steps he returned to the waiting group.

"What's wrong?" Adam sensed a tension, a prescience of dread.

"Tracy says she can't come."

"What!"

"I don't understand it; she's never refused before." Jed

shoved his hands deep into his pockets, angry at his own helplessness.

"Where is she? I'll convince her. Surely she can't refuse to help a little girl."

"No." Halloran's restraining hand on Adam's arm halted his headlong rush through the crowd. "If she says she won't come, nothing you can do or say will change it."

"But why?" Adam looked bewilderedly at the tall dark man who had become his link with sanity in the last hour. "Why wouldn't she come?"

"Who knows?" Jed shrugged. "Usually she's very agreeable and more than willing to help. She works well with us, but no one really knows what's behind those black eyes of hers."

The sound of a heavy motor followed by the screech of brakes and the slamming of many doors interrupted their quiet consultation. More than twenty men and women emerged from two vans and began to set up the paraphernalia of a mobile television newscast. In only minutes cameras were trained on the crowd and the mountain. The newscaster spoke into his microphone in funereal tones.

"We are here, ladies and gentlemen," the reporter said into his microphone, speaking rapidly and dramatically, "at the base of the mountain. Rescue teams are preparing to move out at any moment. There is an air of fear running through the crowd as they stare up at the silent mountain. On the faces of those about me I read terror. Has Shadow claimed another?"

"Carpenter!" In two quick strides Jed was at the speaker's side. He planted himself firmly before him, deliberately using his superior size to intimidate. "Stop that drivel! You can film all you want as long as you stay out of the way. But I won't have you frightening the people with that supernatural claptrap. If I hear one more word of it, or if one member of your crew gets in our way, I'll smash you and your cameras. Is that clear?"

"You can't do that," the smaller man blurted out.

"Watch me." Jed turned back to the rescue teams, dismissing the self-important man with not so much as a shrug. With a quick, appraising eye he checked the readiness of the teams. When all seemed to be in order, and with a curt nod to Adam, he addressed the waiting men. "All right, each of you knows what you're to do. We have a lot of daylight left. Let's make the most of it, and good luck."

"Wait!" a high, shrill voice called from the crowd. "Look, it's Tracy."

As one, the group turned to follow the direction of the boy's thin, gesturing arm. To the west a small cloud of dust moved constantly nearer. A battered jeep jolted over the rough road of the flat valley floor. In hovering quiet all waited.

Adam Grayson watched, his rage rising, for soon he would face the woman who had refused to help in the search for his child.

It seemed an eternity before the aged, dented vehicle reached the crowd, which parted to let it pass. The unblinking eye of the television camera followed her as she braked to a halt a short distance away from everyone. With no flicker of greeting, she pulled a heavy pack from the back of the jeep, then unfolded her five-foot-six frame from beneath the wheel. With a flip of her long dark hair she turned to face Jed Halloran.

Adam realized then that she was older than she first appeared. This Tracy Walker was not a young girl. Her body was slender and strong-limbed. Her hair was swept back into a single braid, its silver-black sheen a marked contrast to the streak of stark white that began at her left temple to interlace with the dark strands. No smile curved her lips. Her solemn face was perfectly symmetrical, with highly arched brows, strong cheekbones, and shadowed hollows that were a photographer's dream. Obsidian eyes stared through a heavy fringe of lashes, equally as dark. Only the slashing scar that began at her forehead and curved downward to meet and blend with the white of her hair marred the smooth texture of her skin. The incongruous first beginnings of laughlines at her eyes softened the too perfect face. Tracy was nearly thirty, and looked every bit of it.

Silently, with only a gesture, she signaled for the dog sitting in the passenger seat to join her. He was coal-black with only tips of silver at his chest to relieve the inky shine of his coat. With the prowling movements of a stalking animal, he eased from the seat and moved to her side.

He was more massive than large. The breadth of his chest recalled an ancestry of beasts of the wilderness. As Tracy walked to join them, he trotted by her, pacing his step with her stride. Silver eyes blazed beneath his canine brow, telling the world he was tame because he chose to be. Wolfe was well named.

"Well, Tracy." Jed stepped forward to meet her. "You changed your mind."

"Yes." No inflection shaded the single word, but it was enough. The husky contralto triggered instant and total recall in the harried mind of Adam Grayson.

As he stared at the calm, self-assured woman before him, he remembered a fresh young actress who had talent, beauty, and had been a rich man's plaything. He had photographed her many times, in many places and many poses. Then at the height of her success, tragedy, death, and scandal had struck and she had disappeared.

Now, nearly ten years later, she stood before him, little changed but for the laughlines, the scar, and the streak of white hair. Adam could not reconcile himself to the fact that she alone held the life of his daughter in her hands.

"Tracy." Jed, by word and nod, drew her into the waiting circle. "This is Adam Grayson. It's his daughter who's lost on the mountain."

"Mr. Grayson." She nodded curtly but no recognition

stirred in her eyes. She turned back to Jed. "What are your plans? Have you divided into sectors?"

Soon both were immersed in talk of schedules, sectors, procedure, and assignments. Tracy listened attentively, offering few comments until Jed addressed her specifically.

"Where will you begin?"

"With the first of the caves, then work my way up."

"The first is unstable and dangerous," Jed muttered harshly, leaving unsaid a dreaded thought.

"Yes. It's all the more reason to get started." She, too, did not speak of the dangers of a cave-in and what it might do to the small child.

"Then you are ready?"

"You all go on. I'd like to speak to Mr. Grayson for a minute. Wolfe and I will be working alone, so I need not start with you." Jed nodded his agreement and with his men moved toward the mountain. Tracy watched as they scattered in the different directions each team was to take. She stared for long quiet moments at the towering mountain, then pivoted gracefully and turned her back on its dark presence. With another subtle motion of her hand she signaled that the dog should remain, and took the few short steps needed to bring her face to face with Adam.

The sun beating down on her gave a golden glow to her dusky skin and lighted her hair with a blue-black iridescence. She was astonishingly lovely. Bile rose in Adam's throat as painful memories assaulted him. Memories of a young dark Tracy intermingled with those of a young blond starlet, equally as talented, equally as lovely, and lost to him forever.

The futile sense of loss, fed by a helpless, hidden panic, turned to resentment. He resented, irrationally, that she was here and well, and that at this moment she was the most important person in his life. The simmering, unreasoning rage spilled over as he virtually attacked her, hating her for being so vibrantly alive.

"So, the prima donna decided to come down from her mountain after all." His snarl took her by surprise, but she did not show it.

Tracy's only response was the lifting of one eyebrow. The other winged brow did not move, but the scar seemed to pull and tauten. Many women might have hidden the angry welt with a sweep of hair, but not Tracy. She accepted it as an inescapable part of herself, and she had learned long ago from a man of great wisdom not to fight what she could not change. It was in this spirit she accepted Adam's anger. She had dealt with frantic people before and understood that worry assumed many forms. For this reason she was tolerant and ignored his attack.

"Was it the lure of the cameras that enticed you here?" he continued, "Do you want to see your face splashed over the screen again? Even older and scarred, it's still a pretty face." Cold rage glittered in his eyes as he raked her with a contemptuous look, despising her beauty even as he acclaimed it.

"I came to help find your child, Mr. Grayson," she answered calmly, standing in a relaxed posture, refusing to give him the fight he was so obviously seeking.

"Of course you did, but not until after the TV cameras and the newsmen arrived. It's been ten long years and you still need the mindless adulation, don't you?" As the bitter, accusing words were spoken, something in the back of his mind recalled Adam to sanity, warning him that he shouldn't be acting this way. Like her or not, he needed this woman. She could easily turn away and go back to her side of the valley, destroying his best hope of finding his child. His thoughts must have been reflected on his anxious face, for the woman before him smiled in quiet understanding.

"I came to help and for no other reason, I assure you, Mr. Grayson. I would prefer that the cameras and the crew were not here." She shrugged lightly, relegating this, too, to that realm beyond her control and accepting it. "But it would seem the news media is an irrevocable part of our lives. I can't trouble myself with them. Your child is my first and only priority."

Something in her tone and her stance told Adam that she meant it. Sincerity and concern were in her eyes, and he realized that he had misjudged her. Weary from the mind-battering tension and uncertainty, his shoulders slumped. He ran his hand over hot, burning eyes, then clenched it into a tight fist to stop its shaking.

"I will find her. Wolfe and I haven't failed yet." Impulsively she touched his arm in a gesture of comfort. She did not add that though they had never failed, they had at times been too late. Always protective of others, she felt a curious and even stronger need to shield this bitter stranger from the horrors that might be.

For the first time, Tracy really looked at the man before her. He was half a foot taller than she, broad of shoulder and narrow-hipped. His shaggy gray hair was shot through with black and was lustrously thick. Wintry-gray eyes stared bleakly at her from a craggy, ashen face. Deep creases lined his mouth but could not destroy its sensual shape. He had about him that closed-in look of a man who had been struck one more mortal blow yet still survived. He hurt, and it was all the more painful because he would not allow himself to show it. Tracy's heart ached for him, and she tightened her hand on his sleeve.

It was easy to forgive him his insults. She had seen and heard it all before. There was even a pattern she had come to expect. The stronger and more capable the man, the more unreasoning and irritable he became when faced with a rare instance of helplessness. Adam Grayson was most definitely a strong and capable man who was unaccustomed to not being in command.

It was not his insults that puzzled her, for she felt that perhaps because of her initial reluctance to come she deserved them. It was their direction that dumbfounded her. Few people remembered her sojourn into acting, and those who did never gave tongue to the memories. It had been a lifetime ago, another time, another place, another person. She had risen quickly, brilliant and unique. Then, in the face of personal tragedy, had withdrawn to be easily and quickly forgotten by a fickle public. She had returned to her beloved mountains to heal, to relearn simple skills, and to resume the life that had been her first love.

None here spoke of her past, and few beyond the insular mountains associated this Tracy Walker with the glamour of Hollywood. None but a stranger whose tension translated through her fingertips an exquisite awareness. She wanted to stroke the deeply etched lines from his brow and bring the brightness back to his sad eyes. She would find his daughter, and pray that it wouldn't be too late.

"What's her name?" Tracy moved her hand down his arm, letting her fingers rest above his clenched fist. It did not occur to her how rare this was, for she seldom touched people.

"Summer." His voice was a rusty sound laced through with the steel of desperate control. "Her name is Summer, after her mother."

"Is Summer close to her mother?"

"Her mother's dead, Miss Walker. She died two years ago."

Again his expression closed. The slight softening she had sensed earlier had gone. Tracy cursed herself silently, aware that she had added more pain to the nearly unbearable burden this man was already carrying. Not a stranger to loving and losing, she recognized that emptiness in the far depths of his eyes. She saw it deepen and darken at the mention of his wife. The loss of this child would be all the greater if the father had invested a double portion of love, that of the mother as well as the child.

"Would you tell me a bit about Summer?"

"She's little, and she's lost. By now she's probably scared out of her wits. What else do you need to know?" he snapped, helpless irritation resurfacing.

"Yes, she is," Tracy said calmly. "It's because she's scared that I want to know something about her. I want to be able to talk to her about familiar things so she won't be frightened of me."

"Why?" A blunt, demanding question.

"Frightened children sometimes hide from strangers in strange places, Mr. Grayson."

"Oh, God. Do you mean she might run away from help?"

"It's been known to happen," she answered softly. As would Jed Halloran, Tracy knew instinctively that Adam would prefer the truth, straight and to the point.

"Yessiree," an old, quavering voice interjected. "I mind the time we looked fer the Talbot boy. Knowed he was about. Found his sign. It was a week fore we got 'im."

"Hush up yore mouth, Ezra Price." A tiny sprite of a woman, gnarled and wrinkled, dressed in a faded print dress and apron, glared up at the thin, cadaverous man. Satisfied that he was properly hushed when he shoved his hands deep into his overall pockets and rocked uneasily back and forth on his heels, she said encouragingly to Adam, "The Talbot boy was afore Tracy come back to the mountains. Her and Wolfe would of made quick work of finding that fool young'un."

Though Adam flinched, he ignored this muttered exchange. Only the harsh hiss of his ragged breathing signaled that he had heard it. He had forgotten the crowd that stood quietly, expectantly, waiting about him. From the moment Tracy had arrived he had concentrated exclusively on her. Despite his hateful sarcasm she had become his anchor. Even now his eyes devoured her, as if wanting to absorb her skills, making them his for his daughter's sake.

"Will you tell me about her?" Tracy repeated, insisting gently as much to distract him as in need to know. She took her hand away from his, aware that a man such as he would not appreciate her knowing how violently he was trembling.

He took a long, harsh breath, then, as if a dam had burst, began to speak. One fact tumbled out after another. Listening intently, Tracy learned that the child was small for her age, but never shy; that she loved to be sung to sleep, but not since her mother died; that she loved the stars and the moon, but hated dark, cloudy nights; that she loved dolls, but her favorite toy was an aged teddy bear.

That she was all he had left of a woman he had loved very much, Tracy thought.

"She doesn't play with Bear anymore," Adam went on. "He's too old and fragile, but he sleeps on her pillow every night." The thought of his little girl, lost and afraid and without her best friend, cast an even chalkier pallor to his face. The skin seemed to pull so tautly, the bones of his finely chiseled jaw grew more prominent and harsher.

"If you will get Bear for me, I'll take him to her." She looked with compassion into his empty steel-gray eyes, hoping she wasn't making an impossible promise. No! She willed herself not to doubt. The child would be found alive and well; she would make it so.

"I have him in the car. I thought if . . . when they found her, she might need him." For the first time his control seemed in danger of breaking. "I'll get him for you."

Turning swiftly, he made his way to the car parked nearby. From the seat he lifted a tattered, faded stuffed teddy bear that had been well loved. One eye was missing; an ear had been chewed until it resembled a cauliflower. A wisp of stuffing protruded from a tiny split in his lumpy belly. One glance and Tracy knew that this was the security the child would need. She took it from Adam gently, holding it much as a little girl would.

"I'll take good care of him and see that Summer has him as soon as possible," she said in a husky voice.

As she moved to her pack to make her last preparations, Adam made a lightning-quick decision. "I'm going with you."

"No."

"Damm it, Tracy. That's my child out there. I can't just sit here doing nothing." The break had come. If he had not been so strong, it would have come long before.

"No." Tracy was adamant. She understood how he felt, but his place was here. "You know you need to be here when they bring her out. If you're with me, what will she think? She's going to want her father. You have to be here for her."

"You're the one who will find her," he said confidently. "If I'm with you, she'll have her father that much sooner."

"You can't go." Tracy shook her head. She couldn't allow him to see what she might find. "I always work alone. You would just be in the way."

"I'm no fool," he snapped. "I wouldn't hinder you."

"You aren't dressed for Shadow."

"I'm dressed as you are." He impatiently swept her slender body with an assessing glance. She wore a heavy cotton shirt tucked snugly into even heavier jeans. A wide belt with a sheathed knife hanging from it circled her small waist. The legs of the jeans were encased by knee-high boots that were laced with leather cords.

"No, Mr. Grayson, you aren't." Tracy turned away, gathering up her pack and her coat. Even in the heat of summer, nights on the mountain would be cold. Moving quickly, before he could ask any more questions, she signaled for Wolfe, and the two of them headed for the dense underbrush at the foot of the mountain. If he asked, she would tell him the truth, but if she could avoid that one question, perhaps he could keep a small portion of his terror at bay.

Adam watched her stride away. Her long legs covered the ground easily. The huge dog trotted by her side. At the forest's edge she turned, waved once, then disappeared into the trees.

"I should have gone with her," Adam muttered under his breath.

"Now, Mr. Grayson, Tracy was right. You ain't dressed right for the mountain," Ezra said in his reedy voice, startling Adam. He had again forgotten the waiting crowds and the cameras.

"I have on jeans like all the others."

"You ain't got no boots, Mr. Grayson," Ezra said laconically.

"Boots?" Adam's tired mind was barely functioning as he looked down at his tennis shoes. "What does that matter?"

"Rattlesnakes."

"Rattlesnakes! Oh, my God."

"Yessiree, I mind that time we kilt one over on Piney Ridge that was seven foot if he was a inch, and big around as a man's arm. That feller had eighteen rattles. Old Billy Simms has that rattle now. He—"

"Ezra, hush up." Again the tiny woman glared up at him as he warmed to his story. "Is yore tongue loose at both ends? Land sakes, you'd scare a body to death with yore wild tales. Just don't you pay him no never mind, Mr. Grayson. Tracy'll find yore little purty, and bring her back to you safe as a bug in a rug."

Rattlesnakes! Adam had sensed that Tracy had avoided telling him something. Rattlesnakes! He stared up at the sun; it had hardly moved at all. He wished this nightmare of a day would end, but was afraid that night would come before Summer was found. It promised to be a hard day no matter what. He looked again toward the trees where Tracy had disappeared.

"Please find her, Tracy," he murmured, not thinking

how incongruous it was to trust so implicitly where only minutes ago he had literally hated. "Please."

Adam's face was desolate as he watched and waited. He was not aware of the comforting hand little Sarah Price placed on his arm.

Two

The sun continued its trek across the cerulean sky, burning away the last of August's morning mists. Its white-hot rays bore down relentlessly, threatening unusual and sweltering temperatures.

"Mr. Grayson," someone said, and Adam accepted the cup of cool water that was thrust into his hand. He drank sparingly, barely assuaging his thirst, his anxious eyes never leaving the mountain. Was Summer thirsty? Was there a spring or a creek she could drink from? Looking in contempt at the cup in his hand, he crushed it, unaware of the blood that mingled with the water that spilled over his fingers and the broken plastic. His gaze returned to the mountain, looking for a sign that wasn't there.

"It shore is hot, ain't it?" Ezra Price squatted by Adam. "Might be a good sign. Them snakes won't crawl in this heat. Instid, they'll lie up in the shade till cool of day."

"Land sakes, Ezra, be still!"

"Now, Sary, I jest wanted to make him feel better." Ezra turned from his wife back to Adam. "Ain't wimmen the beatinest? Marry a little mite of a gal then find out she's all mouth. Talks alla time. Big eater too."

Adam heard the words in the dim recesses of his

mind. Perhaps later, when he was no longer in the grips of this numbing fear, he would appreciate the awkward efforts as a kindness. Then he would chuckle at the absurdity of this loquacious man considering his tiny, nearly silent wife a talker. Perhaps. But not just now. Now he was consumed by the gut-twisting worry that grew with each passing tick of the clock.

As the day continued, other than the TV crew and Melinda, who hovered at the fringes, the only constants were Ezra and Sarah. Sarah had appointed herself Adam's personal guardian. She saw to it that food was brought, offered, and when it was refused by a slight shake of his head, unobtrusively taken away.

Quietly and efficiently she rode herd, guarding her well-meaning husband's tongue and keeping the prying newsmen with their "infernal contraptions" away. None dared cross this miniature myrmidon whose bright green eyes snapped and shone from among the wrinkles and folds left by age and a life of hardships.

As the twilight faded and the first of the night creatures began their song, the rescue teams came slowly in from the mountain. One by one, spent and weary, they walked past Adam. None spoke, but several patted him on the shoulder, despairing shakes of their heads meeting his hopeful gaze. Jed Halloran was last to emerge from the dense underbrush. Adam knew at a glance that he had fared no better.

"Not a trace." Jed stopped before Adam, his face harsh and grim in the purple darkness. "We'll start at first light tomorrow."

"Tracy?"

"None of us saw her. She should be in any minu—" Three shots rang out, echoing through the valley, bounding off the adjoining hills, then sounding again. "She's found her!"

"Thank God!" Unthinking, Adam rushed toward the sound. Jed's hand at his arm stopped him. Clawing at the powerful hold, Adam snarled, "Let me go, damn you. Summer will need me."

"No! Adam, listen to me. We don't know where she is. We can't go up there in the dark; it would be suicide."

"But I heard the shots. They came from the right," Adam protested with a wave of his hand.

"Maybe they did, maybe they didn't. The echo here can play tricks on you. Three shots means Summer's all right. Trust Tracy. She'll bring her out in the morning when it's safer."

Adam recognized the wisdom of his words. He knew Shadow's reputation as treacherous and unforgiving. This time it was giving up its hostage, wrested from it by Tracy. But not until morning. Adam must wait; there was little else he could do.

On Shadow, in the sheltering hollow of a shallow cave, a campfire burned. Flame licked greedily at the dry wood, its light and warmth welcome to the three who sat before it.

Sitting cross-legged, Tracy held a small child in her lap. With her curls and smooth, translucent skin, Summer was beautiful. One small hand clutched the ragged Bear, the other a long dark braid. Tears of fright had long since dried, and she slept trustingly and tranquilly.

At Tracy's knee lay Wolfe, his eyes closed, his breathing labored and stentorian. She buried the fingers of her free hand in the thick dark pelt, stroking him with all the love of a breaking heart. He moved slightly, licked her gently, sighed once, and rumbled a farewell deep in his chest.

Long after he was quiet, Tracy sat with her hand curled at his side, tears streaming down her face. Her choice had been made. There could have been no other. She was certain Wolfe had understood.

* * *

By early morning Adam was pacing ceaselessly over the clearing. He had watched and waited, impatient for each ray of light that had crept with agonizing slowness into the starless sky.

A soft breeze rose with the sun, dancing over the valley floor and weaving among the trees. All was still and quiet but for the murmuring of the tall pines. Then, without warning, Tracy stepped from the shade that clung thickly at the edge of the forest. She walked with a sure and unburdened step into the open field. For a heart-wrenching moment Adam thought she was alone, then he saw that she held Summer in her arms.

"Thank God." It was a low, rasping growl, half whisper, half prayer.

"Daddy!" The sweetest voice he had ever heard was followed by a ripple of happy laughter.

Gently Tracy put her down. The child ran three steps, stopped, whirled to race back again to Tracy, who still knelt in the grass. Short, pudgy arms were wrapped fiercely about her as wet, smacking kisses interspersed with giggles were scattered over her face and a small hand stroked the dark braid. Then, with beloved Bear clutched to her, Summer ran into her father's waiting arms.

"Oh, baby, you scared me," Adam said huskily into the blond ringlets as he nuzzled the tender curve of her neck.

"I was scared, too, Daddy. Until Tracy brought me Bear. It was awful dark and we built a fire in a cave." She paused, then with the truthfulness of the very young, added matter of factly, "Maybe I was still a little bit scared, but Tracy held me and Bear and told us funny stories."

"Did she now? And did she tell you not to ever wander out of the yard again?" Relief warred with sternness, and won.

"I won't, Daddy. Besides, Tracy said you'd worry if I did." Summer kissed his cheek again and presented

Bear for his share of loving. With heavy lids shielding his red-rimmed eyes and dampness on his cheeks, Adam hugged them closely, oblivious to the satisfied murmurs of the crowd.

At the edge of the watching group Silas Carpenter murmured in hushed, somber tones of the averted tragedy, of the skilled and beautiful tracker, and of a valiant life given for another. The cameras searched for and found Tracy.

With a tender smile on her face and a sadness deep in her eyes, she had watched father and daughter reunited. Now she had one last painful service to perform. Even as she turned away Summer was speaking innocently and unwittingly of the death.

"Daddy, after he found me, why did Wolfe go to sleep and not wake up, like Mommy?"

"What?" Adam stared blankly down into Summer's frowning face, her words registering dully in his mind. Then he looked up with compassionate understanding, seeking Tracy. He scanned the meadow, but it was empty. A flash of blue shone among the green trees and he knew that she had returned to Shadow.

"Tracy," Adam called, and, setting Summer on her feet, moved toward the path Tracy had taken.

"Let her go, Adam." Jed Halloran moved to his side. "What she has to do she'd rather do alone."

"You know?"

"I do now. Doc Jacobs, the vet from over at Rockville, stopped by late last night. He told me then. I should have guessed myself when she didn't come instantly."

"But what happened? The dog looked in perfect health."

"He was old, Adam. He was her grandfather's dog long before he was hers. His heart just gave out. This last search was too much for him."

"Then she sacrificed Wolfe for Summer." He held his daughter in his arms once more, stroking her hair.

"She had no choice."

"She could have stayed away."

"She tried and couldn't. Remember?"

The silver and the dark heads both turned toward Shadow. The visible trails were empty, but they knew Tracy was there saying good-bye to an old friend.

Late into the night, long after the well-wishers had departed and his sister had arrived, Adam sat holding a drink in his hand, something he did rarely now. Twice he rose to stand in Summer's doorway to watch her as she slept. How beautiful and peaceful she was with the covers tucked beneath her chin and Bear snuggled next to her cheek.

"Adam? Hadn't you better get to bed? You need some rest." Liza in her robe and nightgown, ready for bed herself, watched her brother worriedly. He had been dreadfully quiet all day. Beneath his jubilant elation hovered a darkness that even Summer's gay chatter couldn't penetrate.

"I think I'll stay up for a while yet. You go on. You must be tired from the trip."

"A bit." Liza accepted defeat. "Good night, Adam."

"Good night. Liza?" Adam waited until she turned back toward him, "I'm glad you're here."

"So am I," she murmured, and left him staring into the amber liquid in his glass.

Adam's thoughts were not of this traumatic day but of days ten years past. As if it were only yesterday he could see raven-haired, black-eyed Tracy and his beloved Sharon, blond and blue-eyed. When both had been very young actresses, a wily agent had astutely assessed the value of their difference. He drew attention to it, exploited it. They were Tracy and Sharon, Sharon and Tracy. And through it all they were never competitors, but friends.

At the height of their success, when Adam and Sharon had just begun seeing each other, disaster overtook Tracy. There was an explosion aboard the yacht of a married producer and she was the only survivor, found hours later clinging to a bit of flotsam and grievously injured. For weeks, as she fought for life, she had been the target of much speculation and sly innuendoes. Then she suddenly dropped from sight without a trace.

Adam had watched as Sharon grieved for her friend. She had denied the rumors and remained staunchly loyal while she searched futilely, hoping each day to hear some word. Later, as her own life took new direction, the hurtful memories of Tracy faded into the background. Blissfully in love, Sharon had turned her back on fame, fortune, and all else Hollywood had offered. To be Adam's wife was all that she asked of life.

They had known eight wonderful years, their happiest day when Summer had been born. Two years ago, after sharing a private dinner for two and the lovemaking that was so special between them, Sharon had fallen asleep in Adam's arms. Sometime in the darkest hour, as quietly and as gently as she had lived, she had died.

The doctors, with blank eyes and somber faces, had muttered complicated gibberish about an undetected congenital weakness, a failing heart, and unavoidable circumstance. But all Adam understood was that Sharon had gone from him. For months he had sought solace in a glass, until Summer's growing need for him pierced the alcoholic fog. Through her trust and faith she gave him cause to put aside his shattered dreams and begin again. With Sharon's child as the center of his life, he had learned to live with his memories. Until today. Until Tracy.

A quiet step sounded on the porch, one that he had waited for all evening. Without looking up, he spoke softly.

"Tracy."

"Yes."

"I knew you would come." He turned to face her. She stood in the doorway, quiet and relaxed with no visible sign of the grief that must be lacerating her. Only the slight tautening of the scar at her temple and a dusting of blue beneath her eyes attested to her fatigue.

"How is Summer?" There was an utter stillness about her that was uncanny.

"Please, come in." He rose as she stepped farther into the room. Indicating a chair with a nod, he watched as she walked across the room. She sat and waited.

Long minutes passed as he absorbed her cool composure. At last he answered. "Summer's fine. Thanks to you and Wolfe."

Only a slight flicker of pain surfaced, and it was hidden quickly behind her mask of control. She said nothing.

"Tracy, can you forgive me for the things I said yesterday?"

"You were upset." He could read no more from the flat, stoic words than from her expression and rigid posture.

"That's hardly an excuse."

"It's happened before. Strong people react pretty much the same." She shrugged, meeting his look squarely. "It will happen again."

"Will there be a next time? Will you track again without Wolfe?"

"I suppose I will, if I'm needed. Adam?" She used his first name easily and comfortably. "How is it that you remembered my past?"

"I was there for most of it." He waited for a reaction. There was none.

She studied him closely, but she had no memory of him. And he was not a man to be forgotten. Surely . . . She shook her head slowly. No! She seldom forgot anymore.

"You don't remember?"

"No." She shook her head again, watching him intently. "I'm sorry."

His eyes moved to the mark at her temple, wondering. "You do remember Sharon?"

"Sharon Summers?"

"Sharon was Summer's mother."

Nothing about Tracy changed. Her face lost none of its serenity. She sat perfectly erect with her hands resting lightly on the arms of the chair. Adam's gaze moved carefully over her until his eyes met and held hers. There he found no tranquility. In their dark depths was a raw, primitive pain that nothing could ease. Tears glittered but did not spill, then were hidden by a sweep of lashes.

"Sharon's dead?" The pain in her eyes was also in her voice.

"Yes."

"Two years ago?" Her voice broke slightly, then was controlled determinedly.

"Yes."

"I lost track of her and couldn't find her, but I liked to think of her living each day well and happy." She raised tortured eyes to his. "Was she happy?"

"We were both happy."

"I'm glad." She was hurting, and Adam wanted to take her in his arms to soothe her as he might Summer.

"Adam, I . . ."

"You still don't remember me," he said gently.

"No."

"There's really no reason you should. We never met officially. I was on the other side of the camera."

"I knew all of Sharon's friends," she said in a low voice.

"Sharon and I hadn't had more than a date or two when you had your accident." He watched as Tracy relaxed visibly. "She searched for you after you left the hospital. Where did you go?"

"To another hospital for therapy, then here to be with my grandfather." Old memories hurt alongside the new.

Adam stepped behind her chair, his hand brushing over her brow, then lightly tracing the scar. "This is from the accident."

She nodded, though it was not a question and needed no answer.

"Were there any lasting effects?" Rhythmically he stroked the jagged ridge.

Wondering how he knew it ached, she relaxed beneath his touch. "For a while. But not anymore. There's an occasional headache, some weakness on the right side. The really bad part was the aphasia."

"Was it severe?"

"Yes."

"You couldn't speak?"

"I could speak as well and as clearly as before." An aura of sadness hovered over her as she seemed to draw away to a distant place of hurtful remembrance. Her voice dropped to a softer tone. "Oh, yes, I could speak very well. Very beautifully enunciated gibberish."

"Did you know?"

"I knew it was gibberish. I *always* knew I hadn't said what I intended." She closed her eyes. "I couldn't find the right words. If I called a house a tree, I knew instantly I'd made a mistake. Then, in searching for the right word, I might call it several things, all of them wrong."

"Did you have trouble understanding?"

"Never. Comprehension wasn't a problem. I understood everything that was said or written. I simply couldn't express myself."

Adam's hand at the scar grew still as he understood the devastating effect of her injuries. What agony for a quick, intelligent mind to be trapped in an injured brain. He wished desperately he could stop the flow of her words, but he knew he must hear her out.

"And now?" he said into the silence that had surrounded them.

"When I'm tired or upset, a word might escape me.

Then sometimes there's some agnosia, which means I don't visually recognize things. It doesn't happen often, and it's usually only fleeting."

"You were afraid you hadn't recognized me."

"For a moment." His soothing touch, the gentle timbre of his voice lulled her into a new and easy trust as she spoke a secret thought. "I don't think I'll ever be free of that fear."

Adam silently acknowledged the depth of her uncertainty. "Why did you come back to the mountain?"

"Familiar surroundings were thought to be beneficial for me. My grandfather brought me here to what I knew best."

"What about therapy? Surely you needed quite a bit."

"I did. Twice a week he took me over the mountains to a medical center. The other days he worked with me."

"Your grandfather must have been quite a man."

"He was. Without him I wouldn't have survived."

"You were still that ill?" He was shocked by her grave words. The thought that she had nearly died, and the waste it would have been, made him angry. It was a strange reaction to something long since resolved.

"My body had healed." She touched the scar, her fingertips brushing his and growing still at the moment of contact. A tension crackled between them, and neither moved until Tracy sighed and continued in a steady voice. "My brain was still bruised and battered."

"The aphasia?"

Tracy nodded. "There's no doubt I would have lived, but without him I would have lost myself."

Her words were calm, too calm. He needed to see her eyes. There he would be able to read the truth. He took his hand from her forehead, stroking it down the length of her hair, then touching her shoulder before moving away. The chair he sat in gave him an unrestricted view of her face, palely lit by the single lamp.

She was beautiful . . . and for the first time in two long years Adam realized how lonely he had been.

"And Wolfe helped you too," he said.

"Yes." It was a murmured half whisper. "And now both are gone."

Adam understood the great depths of her loss. Wolfe had been not only her friend and helpmate in her precarious recovery, he had been her last link with her grandfather as well. Looking into her stark gaze, Adam found himself wishing he had known the man and the dog . . . and the younger Tracy.

As if she knew he could see beneath her brave front, Tracy dropped her head, shielding her eyes. Like thick ebony spikes her lashes lay against her cheeks. She drew a long shuddering breath, then faced him again. Needing to deal with all that hurt and have done with it, she broached pain with pain.

"Can you tell me about Sharon?" she asked, her voice trembling only slightly.

For the first time ever, he found that he could speak of his and Sharon's last moments together. "She died while she slept in my arms. The doctors assured me there was no pain. She simply went to sleep and never woke up."

"I'll miss her," Tracy murmured. "It's strange, isn't it? I hadn't seen her in years, but I'll miss her. You must think me mad."

"No. I understand. I think she felt the same way about you. In fact, she spoke of you often at first. To Sharon you were Tracy Brendon."

"Brendon is my middle name. I chose to use it, rather than Walker, for personal reasons."

"Sharon told me once." He could remember now that long-forgotten conversation.

Tracy moved. It was only a subtle shifting, but she seemed, somehow, at ease. "I'm glad Sharon had you. You loved her. I can hear it in your voice. She deserved that."

"I did love her. I still do."

"I know."

"Have I thanked you, Tracy, for giving me back Sharon's child?"

"There no need for thanks. I did only what I had to do. It was my job, nothing more."

"You knew Wolfe couldn't survive, yet you came."

"A child for a dog? It was not a question of choice, Adam." Another grief she had so neatly filed away broke free, ripping through her, raw, wild, and destructive.

"Would you like to see her?" Adam asked, standing up. "She does look like Sharon, doesn't she?" Like a precious gift, he offered healing succor in the form of his daughter.

"I'd like that." Tracy placed her hand in his and he helped her to her feet.

He led her down a narrow hallway to a door that stood partially ajar. A night light burned, filling the room with a dim glow. Unthreatening gray shadows flickered as a tree outside the open window swayed in the night breeze.

A gentle sigh drew their attention to the child who was nestled among the covers. A chubby hand curled at her cheek, while curls, burnished gold by the lamplight, clung damply to her forehead. Bear, lumpy and tattered, stood guard from his place of honor nearby.

A slight smile curved the tiny lips, then was gone, and she burrowed deeper still into the comforting down of the pillow. Only a long, wicked scratch at her wrist recalled the day, but nothing disturbed her peaceful slumber.

Tracy brushed back a ringlet that had fallen over an eyelid. Her finger was brown and strong against the tender white skin.

Was anything as special or as lovely as a sleeping child? Looking at her now, Tracy acknowledged that Summer did look like Sharon, but it had been Adam's gray eyes that had looked so trustingly at her in a cave on the mountain.

"Thank you, Adam," she said softly. Seeing Summer sleeping contentedly did help to ease the pain.

He bent to kiss Summer's tousled hair, then straightened and looked down at her. She was all that he had left of a wonderful dream.

"Sharon was pregnant when she died," he said softly. It was something he had never told another living soul. The dinner and the loving had been a joyful celebration of the long-awaited confirmation. It had been one more special secret that had been his and Sharon's alone, to keep and to savor for a while. Then it had been too late to share their happiness with the world. He spoke of it now, wanting Tracy to understand how very precious her gift of Summer's life had been.

She neither moved nor spoke, and only by the tears that trickled down her cheeks did Adam know that she had heard. No sob sounded in the stillness, no lines of distress marred her face. Yet hers was an infinite sadness.

"Don't, Tracy." He cupped her chin in one hand, tilting her face to his. With his thumbs he wiped away the tears. "Don't cry for me. I learned long ago not to dwell on tragedy. In that way lies madness. We've both lost special loves, but at least we had them for a while. There are those who never have as much in a lifetime. Put your sorrow behind you, darling, and be happy that we still have Summer."

Tracy stood mesmerized by the soothing murmur of his voice, lulled by the warm comfort of his hands, finding solace in the kindness of his eyes. She had an irrational desire to step into those powerful arms, to nestle her head into his shoulder and cling to his strength. She would ask nothing of him but that he hold her, comfort her. It had been so long, and she had been so alone.

"Adam." It was there, trembling in his name, the need and the bitter loneliness.

Carefully, with all the tenderness in him, he drew her into his arms, enfolding her, burrowing his hand into her hair. He didn't speak; he simply let her draw from him the comfort she sought.

Tracy rested her head against his chest, the strong, even beat of his heart sounding in her ear. Its steadiness soothed her. Soon her ragged breathing slowed, then resumed a more natural pace. Her tenseness vanished, and with it the numbing fatigue. She was grateful when his fingers again found the scar at her temple and stroked away a bit of the pain that was pounding there. Warm and secure and, for a time, unburdened by her cares, Tracy sank further into the contentment so freely given. Gradually her eyelids drooped, then closed.

Adam felt the slight relaxing of her body. In one smooth motion he lifted her and carried her to the aged rocker by Summer's bed. Lowering himself into it, he settled Tracy on his lap. A handmade afghan lay on a dresser nearby. He slipped it from its folds and drew it over her to guard against the creeping chill.

She stirred, but only to snuggle closer.

"Better?" he murmured.

Tracy only nodded, her eyes still closed.

She didn't move again as he held her much as she had held Summer the night before. He rested his head against the silk of her hair, breathing deeply of its fragrance. Outside, a night bird sang and then another, and Adam's eyes closed in sleep.

In the first morning hours a figure appeared in Summer's doorway. Liza, her cap of short dark red curls disheveled, looked long and curiously at the sleeping couple.

Driven from her bed by concern for Adam, she had wandered through the house seeking him. She wasn't surprised to find him sleeping by Summer's bedside. It was Tracy who was unexpected.

Having arrived in the midst of the jubilant celebration, Liza had heard repeatedly from one source after another of the loss, of the fear, of the search and the rescue. She had heard far too much of the skilled and heroic tracker not to recognize the dusky-skinned woman who slept so peacefully in Adam's arms.

Tracy was curled in his lap as if it were her true and rightful place. Her hair spilled in an ebony cascade over his hand, which rested at her neck. His arm was pressed against her breast near the open throat of her blouse. With the easy rise and fall of her breathing, the rippling cloth displayed a hint of shadowed cleft and softly rounded fullness.

Moving soundlessly on bare feet, Liza crossed the room. She picked up the fallen afghan from the floor and drew it about them. Neither woke. She waited, watching them for a minute, struck by the contentment on Adam's face. It was a look she had thought she would never see again.

Liza turned her gaze back to Tracy. She saw maturity rather than gay, young innocence; straight dark hair rather than golden curls; dark skin rather than alabaster; an exotic slenderness rather than voluptuousness. There was a strength about her that would complement that of the man who held her.

Tracy was none of the things that Sharon had been. But Adam had had his Sharon. He did not need another.

Adam shifted in his sleep. His hand slipped to curl possessively about a full breast, and Liza smiled a slow, pleased smile. Then, as quietly as she had come, she left them.

The brilliant glow of the sunrise woke him as it crept over the room. Disoriented, he watched as the shadows lost their darkness, faded, then vanished. He was alone and his arms were strangely empty.

"Tracy!"

He sat up abruptly, spilling the afghan that had been

neatly tucked about him onto the floor. His voice was husky with disuse as he called her name.

The tantalizing aroma of rich coffee wafted through the house. Thinking that he might find her there, he hurried to the kitchen.

"Tracy?"

"She's gone, Adam."

He whirled to face Liza, who emerged from her bedroom dressed in jeans and a pale lavender sweatshirt. Her red hair was neatly brushed.

"When did she go?"

"I don't know," Liza said. "She was still with you when I checked around one o'clock. When I woke later, she was gone."

"It was Tracy who found Summer," he said as if it might answer any questions she would ask.

"She's an unusual woman."

"Yes."

"And beautiful."

"I know." He stood at the window staring down the road Tracy would have taken. Almost to himself he murmured, "I had forgotten what it was like to hold a woman in my arms."

"It's time you had a woman in your life, Adam."

"I think maybe you're right," he agreed softly, never taking his gaze from the dusty road.

Three

The sun had risen well into the sky before Tracy moved, then it was only to flip a stray lock of hair over her shoulder. For hours she had sat on a huge outcropping of granite that projected from a mountainside. With her knees bent and her chin resting on her folded arms she had seen the birth of a new day.

Far below, down a narrow ribbon of twisting road, was Adam's sturdy cabin. Where was he? Had Summer awakened to begin her day? Would she ever see them again, Sharon's lovely child and Adam?

Disturbed by her thoughts and uneasy with her memories of the night, Tracy rose restlessly, stretching her long legs and flexing her cramped shoulders. For a long while she stood at the edge of the stone. A light breeze caressed her face and the sun kissed her cheeks. Here on the mountain she had found peace. What could she find in the valley in Adam's arms? She shivered and turned away, not yet ready to deal with the question.

Tracy forced her mind from the haunting thought as she deliberately turned her eyes to Shadow. Wolfe lay there close beside her grandfather. He had been old and tired and had stayed with her far past his time. Now he was at rest. She would miss him and be lonelier.

"It's time to go home, Tracy," she murmured aloud.

"You can't put it off any longer." She had to fight the dread of facing the familiar places without her friend and loving companion. When her grandfather had died, the grief had nearly destroyed her. But she knew that this time she was stronger and could face the sorrow and the memories. Brushing back her hair and looping it in a loose knot, she retraced her steps to the jeep parked at the roadside. Not allowing herself to look at the empty seat beside her, she revved the engine to life, reversed, then headed down the incline toward home.

Tracy's days assumed a pattern. She rose early from an often sleepless night, did her household chores, tended her small garden, then with her sketch pad under her arm, tramped the fields and the forest. Sometimes she stopped to sketch a bit, sometimes not. Some days she remembered to eat the sandwich she always dutifully packed, some days she didn't. She never returned before dusk, always weary, always spent, hoping to find rest in oblivion.

Tracy lost count of the number of times she looked for Wolfe or turned to speak to him. Every part of her day seemed to bring some thought of him.

As she sat by the creek bank, her memories turned to a young and playful Wolfe who forgot his majestic dignity long enough to chase and tease the fish that darted in and out of the submerged stones. Waiting for a prickly porcupine to waddle across her path, she recalled his look of chagrin when he had chosen to annoy one just as prickly and in no mood to play. She had never seen such outraged pride as when she had dug the broken quills from his snout. While she gave right of way, most respectfully, to a band of prissy skunks, she remembered how he had laughed at her and disdainfully turned his nose away when she had run afoul of one of the pungent striped creatures.

Tracy knew that the people of the valley had stood in

awe of Wolfe, believing his prowess as a tracker to be a supernatural skill. She had heard the whispers that called him strange, a phantom with mythical powers, a devil dog. How shocked they would have been if they could have seen his gentleness and his humor. Wolfe had been a capricious creature at times, gay and charming, teasing her in an almost human fashion, yet always savagely protective because he loved her.

She could not escape the memories of the great dog. They were everywhere around her, woven into the fabric of her life.

Slowly and by degrees she learned to accept her loss, and each day she missed Wolfe less. It was Adam who was constantly in her mind. The craggy, roughhewn features, the shaggy hair that was the exact color of his eyes, and the gentle smile that curved his lips haunted her thoughts and her dreams. In anger she would chide herself for acting like a giddy young girl and bury herself in her work.

"Hi, Tracy," Jed Halloran called as she stopped her jeep in front of the post office. "Haven't see you in a while."

"Yeah, I know." She jumped to the ground, waiting as he crossed the street to her.

"How have you been?" In his concern, Jed rested a hand on her shoulder, bending his head to look down into her upturned face. Tracy knew what he was asking.

"I'm all right, Jed. Every day it gets a little easier."

"Can I do anything to help?"

"No." She shook her head. "It's something I just have to accept."

"Have you thought about getting another dog?"

"No!" The word whipped from her with a harsh vehemence. As soon as she said it she wished she could recall it. Jed meant no harm, only kindness. She grasped his sleeve, her eyes pleading for forgiveness. "I'm sorry, Jed.

I didn't mean to snap. It's just that there could never be another Wolfe."

"I know." He covered her hand with his. "There's a nice way you could apologize to me."

"Oh, yeah?" Laughter was in her voice, answering the chuckle that rumbled beneath his words.

"There's a barn dance over at the MacFarlands tomorrow night. Come with me."

"You know I don't dance, Jed."

"Doesn't matter. I'll just spend the evening looking at you."

"Idiot." Tracy laughed again. "Okay, you win. I'll go."

"Great. I'll pick you up early. How about five?" At her agreement he kissed her cheek and patted her shoulder in a brotherly fashion. "Wear something sexy so the other guys will wish they were me."

Tracy was still laughing as she turned to enter the post office.

"Land sakes," she was greeted when she stepped inside. "Where you been, Tracy? Ain't seen you in a coon's age."

"Hi, Lucy. I've been round and about. Any mail for me?"

"Got another of those letters from that art place in New York."

"Drat! I wish they'd take no for an answer."

"Them lowlanders is persistent, that's fer sure."

"Well, they can just be persistent. I don't intend to leave these mountains, nor send my work." She dropped the offending letter into the trash bin by the door. "See you next week, Lucy."

"Yeah." The large woman chuckled. "To pick up your next letter from those city folk and drop it in the trash again."

"Maybe someday they'll realize that I mean it when I say no, and give up. 'Bye, now." The door banged shut behind her.

"Hello, Tracy."

"Adam!" In her gay chatter with Lucy, she had very nearly run him down. She stopped abruptly, looking up at the fascinating man. "How are you? How is Summer?" The words tumbled from her in a mad, nervous rush. Even if she tried, she couldn't have broken away from his piercing gaze.

"We've both been fine." His eyes released hers as his keen gaze traveled over her body, dwelling on the narrow hips, which looked even narrower than before. "You've lost weight."

"Only a bit."

"Have you been ill?" His voice was terse as concern leaped into his face, and his eyes moved to the scar.

"I've been very well, Adam," she answered firmly with a tinge of an old defensiveness returning. "Just busy."

"I know. I had hoped to see you before now. I came to your cabin several times but never caught you home."

"Was there something special you wanted?"

"I . . . Summer wanted to see you."

"Oh." Disappointment lanced through her and, on its heels, anger. How stupid to be so vulnerable to a man whom she had seen a grand total of three times. One that, once he had finished his research on Shadow, she would most likely never see again. "Summer's well?"

"Yes."

"You already told me, didn't you?" With an agitated hand she pushed the heavy wealth of her hair farther back off her shoulder. It was little more than a nervous reaction.

"Why did you leave me, Tracy?" His eyes had darkened; a frown creased his features.

She made no pretense of not understanding him. "I thought it best to leave while I had a bit of my dignity still intact. I don't make a habit of sleeping in strange men's arms."

"I know that." With the back of his hand he caressed her cheek. "We aren't strangers. We never were."

"Adam—" She stopped, her eyes closed as he traced the line of her jaw with his fingertips.

"Adam, what?" He stepped closer, his voice sinking to a low, musical whisper. "What is it you want, Tracy?"

"I . . ." A fragrance drifted about her, wrapping her in a cocoon of his cologne. It was a clean, woodsy scent that would forever remind her of Adam. Unable to think with him so near, she stepped back, away from his touch, breaking the hypnotic spell. "Nothing, Adam. I have to go."

"No!" His hand at her arm stopped her. "Don't run away from me again. We need to talk."

"What is there left to say? Your daughter was lost. Wolfe and I helped to find her. We *are* hardly more than strangers." Tracy made the point again, this time emphatically.

"Whether you make a habit of it or not, you did sleep in my arms. That makes us a bit more than strangers."

"I was tired. I hadn't slept," she defended herself curtly.

"I know, darling." Again he lifted his hand, this time to stroke the scar. It was as if, in some curious way, he understood that in times of tension or stress the pain could be excruciating. "Was it terrible for you on the mountain?"

"No." Her eyes were held by his. She couldn't look away. "I knew that Wolfe would die there."

"That can't have made it any easier. The people here have told me how he was your constant companion while you were ill. Sarah told me that he seldom left your side."

"Except for my grandfather, he was all that stood between me and insanity."

"Sarah said that your grandfather let you roam Shadow, and that sometimes you got lost."

"I had to have that freedom. Grandfather understood. I was never in any danger. Wolfe always found me."

"Are you lonely without him?"

"Yes." Even the simple word hurt. "Is it foolish to miss a dog like this?"

"Not one who has meant so much to you. Perhaps he did possess those magical powers the villagers hint about."

"No. His only power was love."

"Sometimes I think love has magical powers," he murmured almost to himself, and again he stepped closer. "Tracy . . ."

"Hey, are you two going to stand here all day blocking the doorway?" Jed was standing on the lower step, grinning a friendly greeting. "How are you, Adam? And how's that sweet little charmer?"

"Summer's fine, Jed."

"And the cute little redhead?"

"Liza?"

"Yeah. The gossips say she's your sister."

"For once the gossips have it right," Adam said with a laugh. "She's my kid sister."

"It's plain to see who got all the looks in the family, and it isn't you, my friend." Jed clapped him on the shoulder with a hearty laugh. "You are going to bring her to the dance tomorrow, aren't you?"

"I hadn't thought about it."

"You have to! Can't visit the mountains without attending at least one genuine barn dance. And besides, we wouldn't want that fire-topped city gal to miss her chance at dancing with the master I'll expect you." He grinned confidently. "And you I'll see about five, dark eyes."

With a playful tug of her braid and a jaunty wave to Adam, Jed moved on into the post office.

"You're going with Jed?" The warmth in Adam's eyes had been replaced by a glacier coldness.

"Yes."

"Perhaps I'll see you there." He turned away, dismissing her as if she suddenly no longer mattered.

Tracy could only stare, confused by the lightning-swift change. One minute he had been kind and considerate, almost like a lover, then the next he was coldly aloof and distant. She had no idea what she might have done, but watching his stiff, retreating steps take him farther away from her she knew that she couldn't let him go.

"Adam?"

He slowed only slightly and did not stop. Nor did he acknowledge her call.

"Adam, wait!" Tracy rushed to catch him. For a moment she tried to pace her stride with his, but she was no match for his long legs and could not keep up. He seemed to realize that she couldn't and stopped to look down at her, his face closed and expressionless.

"Well?" The curt word was a demand.

"Hey, look, I don't know what I said that made you so angry. Whatever it was, I'm sorry."

"Why didn't you tell me you were Halloran's property?"

"What?" She looked at him incredulously.

"I said—"

"Never mind," she interrupted, bristling with anger. "I heard what you said. I don't know where you get your ideas, but I can assure you that I'm nobody's property! Nobody owns me. They never have, they never will."

"You're going to the MacFarlands with him."

The man's jealous! Tracy was speechless with the discovery. She looked into the glowering face and did not know if she should laugh, be angry, or feel flattered. One part of her wanted to slap away his arrogance, while another wanted to reassure him and melt the frost in his eyes. Later she wouldn't remember making the decision.

"There's nothing between Jed and me, Adam." She deliberately kept her voice steady with no inflection. "He's a friend, nothing more."

"But you do go out with him."

"Occasionally," she acknowledged. "We enjoy each other's company. The valley's not exactly overrun with single people, you know. Through the years we've just sort of teamed up for some of the parties and the dances."

He relaxed visibly, then a slow, rueful grin spread over his face. "I've been acting like a fool, haven't I?"

"Truth?"

"Of course."

"Then yes. Yes, you have acted like a great, hulking fool," she answered firmly.

"Ouch!" He winced in mock hurt. "You don't mince words, do you?"

"If you don't want to know, don't ask."

His shout of laughter startled her and turned many heads. More than one pleased smile was hidden quickly as one matchmaker after another made note of the couple. A few even nodded their approval when Adam flung an arm about Tracy's shoulders and hugged her to him.

"Arguing is thirsty work. How about a cool drink? I'll buy. In fact, when I left, Summer had just talked Liza into making a fresh pitcher of lemonade, and I have it on the best authority that Aunt Liza's lemonade is t'rrific." The warm laughter was back in his eyes. Tracy could almost fool herself into thinking she had only imagined his swift withdrawal and the hint of a sneer that had hovered beneath the cutting words.

Adam was a man of hidden emotions. He would bear watching and would, indeed, take some careful understanding. Tracy filed the thought away, intending to think about it later. For now she put it aside and smiled her acceptance.

"A tall cool drink would be grand. I had planned to stop by to see Summer anyway."

"Good. I have another errand to do. Why don't you go on ahead and spend some time with her. She's hardly spoken of anything but you for weeks. I won't be long."

Hardly more than a few minutes later Tracy slipped

from her jeep and stood watching Summer while she played under a tree that shaded both yard and cabin. As patches of sunlight broke through the swaying leaves, her bright hair was a poignant reminder of Sharon. Tracy could see why she was life itself to Adam.

"Hello, Summer." Tracy stepped farther into the yard.

"Tracy!" The small child flew across the lawn into her arms. "I kept hoping and hoping you'd come."

"Was there some special reason?" Tracy brushed back the curl that Summer had unsuccessfully tried to push from her face.

"Nope. I just wanted to see you. I told Aunt Liza all about you and Wolfe and the cave and the campfire. She said she'd like to meet you. I told her she couldn't meet Wolfe 'cause he went to sleep like mommy and didn't wake up."

"Summer! You're chattering like a magpie. Slow down." A petite woman who was obviously Adam's sister crossed the lawn toward them. She wiped her hands on the apron that was tied around an impossibly small waist, then grasped both of Tracy's firmly. "I'm Liza, Tracy. I hoped I'd get the opportunity to thank you for all you did for our little rascal here. I don't know what Adam would have done if things had turned out differently. It's not something I like to think about."

A bell-like laugh sounded as she gestured toward some chairs clustered in the shade of the tree. "Gracious, I'm as bad a chatterer as Summer. Come, sit down. I'll get you something to drink. Will lemonade be all right?"

"Lemonade will be fine," Tracy answered, appreciating the sparkle and flair of the young woman. She wasn't beautiful in the strictest sense of the word, but with her coloring and spirit she would be unforgettable. Quite suddenly Tracy found herself thinking of Jed. Liza would be perfect for him. Then just as suddenly she realized she had succumbed to the favorite pastime of the hill women: matchmaking. Heaven forbid that she should be so presumptuous. And yet . . .

"Here we go." Liza set a pitcher and a tray of cookies on the table before them. "Sit. These are pretty good cookies, if I do say so myself. Sit, Tracy, sit."

"Thank you, Liza." Tracy could hardly keep from smiling, for Liza sounded just like Sarah. Oh, Jed, watch out, she thought. Your number has just come up. That thought defeated her. The smile blossomed into a full-blown laugh.

"I said something funny?" Liza asked, looking at Tracy curiously.

"No." Tracy fought to compose herself. "I was just enjoying the day and the company."

"Oh, I see." Liza looked doubtful, but she was far too well-mannered to question anymore.

"Tracy?"

"What, pumpkin?"

"Did Daddy come to your house and tell you to come see me?" Summer reached for a cookie with grubby hands, ignoring the wet cloth Liza had laid by her place.

"I did see your dad, but I was coming to see you anyway."

"Why?" Adam's gray eyes looked at her solemnly from Summer's face.

"I have something for you."

"A present?" An excited smile began to tilt the innocent mouth and there was a happy eagerness in her every feature.

"Umm-hmm." Tracy smiled as she drew a small package from her carryall. It was wrapped in a brilliant yellow paper and tied with a strand of white yarn.

"Can I open it now?" Summer clutched it tightly in her lap.

"Sure you can. Presents are to open, aren't they?"

Summer needed no other invitation. With the glee of an energetic six-year-old, she tore the paper away from the box. When she lifted the lid she grew very quiet and still.

"Don't you like it, Summer?"

"Is it real?" She turned her wondering gaze to Tracy.

"No, it's a carving made out of wood."

"Can I touch it?"

"Of course you can. See?" Tracy lifted the tiny blue butterfly from its wrappings. "Since it's wood, it isn't nearly so fragile as a real one would be."

"Did you catch it?"

"No, honey. When I was a little girl, I liked the blue butterfly too. My grandfather carved this for me when I was just about your age."

"It's for me?" Summer asked wistfully. "I can really keep it?"

"You surely can. I can't think of another person I'd rather have it."

"Hi, how are my girls?" Tracy started at the sudden sound of Adam's voice. He was standing in the bright sunlight, smiling at the three of them. Tracy's heart lurched at the vibrant strength that seemed to emanate from him.

"Daddy!" Summer jumped from her chair and rushed to him, carrying the carving like a precious treasure. "Look what Tracy brung me."

"Brought, darling." Adam corrected her as he lifted her high into his arms.

"Look what Tracy brought me," the child repeated dutifully, displaying her gift proudly to her father.

"Ah, that's nice, Summer."

"It's all right, you can touch it. It's not real. Tracy's grampa carved it for her when she was six too. She liked blue butterflies then."

"I'll bet she didn't chase one up on Shadow and lose herself like somebody else I know," Adam teased as he kissed her.

"I won't do that again, Daddy." Summer's eyes were studiously serious.

"I know you won't, baby. I was just teasing." Adam set her on her feet and turned to Liza. "Could I have a drink too?"

"Of course, Adam. Come along, Summer. You can get out the ice for me." Liza offered her hand to the child.

"Okay. I'll leave my butterfly here till I get back." With great care she set the carving down and skipped away to join her aunt.

Adam looked down at the figure and traced the shape of a delicate wing with a broad finger. "Are you sure you want to give this away? It must be very special to you."

"I have others. I'd like Summer to have it."

"I know she'll take care of it. Thank you, Tracy." He turned to look toward Shadow. "At least something pretty has happened to her here at this godforsaken mountain."

"What happened to Summer was not the mountain's fault." Tracy's voice was firmly controlled, seeking with calmness to stem the rising rage she could sense in him. "It's an inanimate object and only what people make of it."

"You don't believe that any more than I do. That pile of rocks damn near killed my daughter and it did kill your dog. At first I thought all the stories I'd heard about it were exaggerated, but I don't now."

Tracy stood to face him, her hand resting on the back of the chair. "Shadow is just like anything that's different. People don't understand it so they look for reasons for the differences, and they don't always make sense. There are good stories about it, but they're not nearly so exciting to gossip about."

"There's nothing good about that thing. It sits there like the knell of doom, waiting to snatch some poor soul away. How you people can live here is beyond me. If I weren't committed to this book, I wouldn't take a picture or write a single word about it."

"I hate to see you misunderstand how we feel about Shadow. For every tale of horror there's some good.

Haven't you discovered that those of us who live here love Shadow just as much as we hate it? Doesn't that prove something?"

"No." When she shook her head, discouraged by his stubborn refusal to listen to reason, he relented. He took her hand in his, staring down at the long, slender fingers as his thumb caressed her palm. "All right, Tracy. Show me this good and pretty mountain. Spend some time with me and let's explore the legends together. Show me your Shadow."

"I don't know, Adam—"

"You've made your claims, now prove them."

He was issuing a challenge. Tracy had never backed down from a dare in her life, but just now all she could think about was how comforting it was to feel the warm, hard hand holding hers.

"Are you afraid, Tracy?" he taunted, leaning down until the loose tendril of hair at her ear was fanned by his breath. "Are you afraid that you can't prove your point, or are you afraid of me?"

"Don't be ridiculous. Why should I be afraid of you?"

"Not of me, Tracy, but of this attraction that's between us. You know as well as I do that there's something there. Are you afraid to find out what it is?"

"We were talking about Shadow." Tracy futilely tried to curb the shiver that rushed through her. His eyes seemed to hold her captive. She wanted to look away, but did not.

"Um-hm," he murmured as he lifted her palm to his lips. "You had something to prove to me, didn't you?"

"Adam . . . no."

"Didn't you?"

"I—all right."

"You won't regret it, darling." He pressed three lingering kisses to her fevered skin, and smiled.

"Daddy! You almost knocked my butterfly off the table." Summer's plaintive cry broke the spell he had cast about her.

*   *   *

Many hours later Tracy paced the floor of her cabin. An angry frown marred her smooth forehead. She had been fuming since she realized how neatly she had been manipulated.

"Damn you, Adam Grayson. You tricked me."

She had been well on her way home before the truth had hit her. Adam was far too intelligent to think a mountain evil or to believe the ugliness some liked to spout about Shadow. It had been an act, she was sure of that. But for what purpose? What earthly reason would he have for lying to her, pretending something that was untrue?

"He pegged you right from the first, Miss Tracy," she said aloud. "He knew that if he made it sound like a dare, you'd jump at the chance to prove yourself right. Fool!"

If Tracy were to face the truth, she would have had to admit that she was angrier at herself than at Adam. There had been no contest, but he had been the winner all the same. He had issued a challenge, and she had given him the victory by accepting.

Furious as she was, Tracy knew she would not back down. She never had; she never would. It was the sort of determination that had kept her injuries from destroying her, and it was what made her a good tracker as well. She never gave up. That in itself was victory of a sort.

When the anger had at last worn itself out, Tracy lay in her bed. She stared out the window at the moonlit world, but saw none of the familiar hills or fields. A broad-shouldered man with a wicked smile was the center of her thoughts.

"Go away, Adam. I want to sleep," she muttered as she drew the sheet under her chin and shut her eyes. Determinedly she kept them closed, but it was quite a while before she truly slept.

Four

The sun had long since slid behind the mountain and the lanterns strung through the leafy oaks were glowing in the twilight by the time Jed and Tracy arrived at the MacFarland farm. Music and voices blended into a low murmur punctuated by the shouts and laughter of children.

"It's not exactly five o'clock, is it?" Jed said, grinning at Tracy. He stepped from the open side of his jeep and walked around it to offer Tracy a hand. "Unpredictable hours are all part of the territory that goes with the job. I wouldn't have kept you waiting if I could have avoided it."

"Hey, Tracy," a young boy called as she passed him. "Someone was looking for you earlier."

"Who, Rick?" She stopped, turning slightly, her eyes searching through the crowd for the man who had disrupted her sleep the night before.

"A little girl. The one who was lost up on Shadow a few weeks back."

"Summer."

"Yeah. That was her name."

"Did she say what she wanted?" Tracy fought down a twinge of disappointment that it wasn't Adam who had asked for her.

"Nah. She just asked us if we'd seen you. They were over on the other side of the dance floor."

"Want to go over?" Jed asked. He, too, scanned the crowd, and Tracy wondered if he was seeking Liza.

"I doubt they're still there now," Tracy said. "Why don't we wait? We're bound to see them before the evening's over." She only hoped Jed was convinced by her nonchalance.

"Then let's sit for a while and watch the fun."

"Sounds good. I left our blanket in the jeep. I'll go get it."

"No need. Not when we have the perfect seats right here." Before she could answer, Jed had swung her high onto the tall stone wall that wound through the Mac-Farland property. Built many years ago, when stone and manpower were plentiful and wire was rare, it still served to mark boundaries and fence the numerous dairy cattle that grazed the rolling green pastures.

"What do you think?" He pulled himself up beside her and grinned down at her. "Beats a blanket, doesn't it?"

"A trifle harder but the view's better."

"An old mountain gal like you can take it. You've been rock-sitting for years. In fact, early one morning a couple of weeks ago I thought I saw you up on Raven's Roost."

"You did," Tracy said, remembering as if it were yesterday the morning she had left Adam's arms. "I had some thinking to do."

"Something important?"

"Maybe."

"Tracy." Suddenly Adam was standing by her side, magnificent in the traditional dress of the dance. His white shirt with the sleeves turned back was a stark contrast to his suntanned skin. In the dim light his hair looked almost black again—until he moved and the heavy strands caught a moonbeam. His face was a study of deeply carved shadows and she could read nothing there as he turned toward her companion. "How are you, Jed?"

"Can't complain, Adam. Things going all right with you?" After an answering nod Jed continued pleasantly. "I hope you haven't come this evening without your beautiful women folk."

"No." Adam's eyes were again on Tracy. "Liza and Summer stopped to speak to Hester Calton."

"Do you think your sister would think I'm rude if I went over and introduced myself?"

"I'm sure she wouldn't." Adam seemed to draw himself from distant thoughts. "Summer would like to see you too. You go on. I'll see to Tracy."

"Okay?" Jed hesitated, having the good grace to feel a bit embarrassed that he was about to desert Tracy when he had very nearly coerced her into coming with him.

"I'll be fine, Jed," Tracy assured him, looking into Adam's half-hidden face as intently as he looked at her. Neither saw the quizzical glance Jed gave them.

In the stillness that seemed to surround them, Adam's gaze lingered on the peach-colored flush that stained Tracy's cheeks, then moved on to her lips, seeming to memorize their shape. As if to test their softness, one finger touched them, then was gone.

At the instant of contact, a current of pleasure caught at her, halting her breath, suspending her in another time, another place, banishing the meadow and its people. There was no crowd, no Jed, no Liza, no Summer. There was only Adam, a stranger she had known and waited for all her life.

The shock of her thoughts drew from her a sharp gasp of surprise, its sound breaking his mesmerized gaze from her parted lips. A swift and deep inhaling of a new breath drew his eyes to the rounded fullness of her breasts. For the space of a heartbeat he smiled his appreciation of her womanliness.

With the uncanny acceptance that was hers, Tracy waited, hardly moving, as Adam's gaze roved over her, missing nothing. He was totally absorbed in her, yet she felt not the least bit uneasy by his searching contemplation.

"You're a beautiful woman, Tracy Walker," he said, stepping closer and stroking her brow with the back of his hand. His voice sank to no more than a hint of a whisper. "The most beautiful woman I've ever seen."

"No more beautiful than you."

"Men aren't beautiful." His low laughter was like a kiss.

"You are." Her grave reply left no doubt that she meant every word.

"Don't, Tracy. Don't look at me like that. Not now, not here." Unaware of what he did, he tucked back a bone pin that had escaped from the dark coil of hair resting at the nape of her neck. His fingers paused at the pulse that beat raggedly at the line of her jaw, then curved to frame her chin, lifting her face to the moonlight. In a voice harsh with strain, he said almost to himself, "I think it might be best if we join Jed and Liza for a while."

He stepped back and waited. She clasped his proffered hand, needing no aid to leave the stone wall but seeking his touch. With fingers interlaced, they joined the others. They had just sat down when Melinda approached them shyly. "Mr. Grayson?" she said.

"Hello, Melinda," Adam said. "Are you enjoying the dance?"

"Yes, sir. Mr. Grayson . . . I was wondering . . . I thought . . ." They could see the girl gather her courage, then she spoke in a rush. "Would it be all right if I take Summer over to play the games? I'd take very good care of her. Truly I would."

"Where are they?"

"Over by the barn there are stalls like this one," Tracy explained, "with bingo, toss-a-penny, darts, that sort of thing. Noah Hawkins will probably be there telling stories too. Later the little ones will sleep in the hayloft until their parents are ready to go. She will be well supervised, Adam."

"And I'll help," Melinda added, wanting to make amends and to acquit herself of the guilt she felt. "I promise I won't let Summer be lost again."

"I know you won't, Melinda," Adam assured the girl kindly. He was rewarded with a tremulous smile. "If Summer would like to go . . ."

"You bet!" The child hopped down from her chair, eager to join in the fun. With a wet smack of a kiss planted somewhere in the vicinity of her father's ear and a wave to the others, she raced away hand in hand with Melinda.

In the silence that followed, Tracy's smile was equally as tremulous as she looked gratefully at the man sitting across from her. Both ignored the sounds of the band striking up another rousing square-dance.

"Liza," Jed said, flicking a knowing glance at the two, "is that our song they're playing?"

"Why, Jed." A pleased chuckle accompanied her answer. "I do believe it is." Not bothering with words of parting that would go unheard, they left to join the dancers.

"That was a thoughtful thing to do," Tracy said above the noisy voices and the music that surrounded them. "Melinda's been heartsick for weeks, worrying about what happened to Summer. Trusting her as you have tonight will help to ease some of her guilt."

"I never meant that she should shoulder all the blame," Adam said.

Tracy's hand closed over his where it rested on the rough boards of the table. Her thumb caressed his knuckles. "You're a nice man, Adam Grayson. The nicest I've ever known. Sharon was a lucky woman."

"Thank you, Tracy." Adam was silent for a long while, his thoughts on times past and faraway places. Though the memories were deeply ingrained and unforgettable, they had at last begun to fade because of this woman whose touch warmed him. His lips relaxed in a hint of a smile as he turned his hand up to catch her fingers in his own. "Let's walk a bit and you can tell me more about all this. Surely it's not the customary barn dance."

Later, as Tracy led him from one booth to another, showing him the crafts on display, she answered his question. "You were right. This is actually more a church social than a dance. We gather here fairly often during the year. Usually it's to raise funds for some cause. This time we hope to earn enough to replace the organ in the church."

"Do you always have it here at the MacFarlands?"

"Always." She smiled. "Look, there's Noah Hawkins. He spends a part of every social telling the legends. The children know them nearly as well as he does, yet they always listen as if it's the first time. Would you like to go over and listen?"

"Not tonight." The look he turned to her was teasing, yet tender. "Tonight my mind's far too filled with music and moonlight, and an entrancing woman."

As color rose in Tracy's cheeks he laughed and drew her to the next exhibit. Stringed instruments, carefully handcrafted in wood, were lined against the wall.

"What are these?"

"They're Clayton Tarleton's dulcimers. Listen." Tracy struck the taut strings with the leather-covered hammer, sounding only a few notes. "Pretty, isn't it?"

"Can you play?"

"Not the dulcimer. The guitar's always been my favorite."

"Will you play for me, darling?" He stepped closer, his head inclined as he waited for her answer.

"Yes, Adam." Tracy stared up into eyes that shone with a strange light. "Someday I will."

In that stolen moment, amid the revelry and jostled by the crowd, he wasn't sure what it was he asked, nor she what she had promised. But both knew it was far more than a song.

"Well, land sakes! Are you two going to stand over there lollygaggin' all evening? Or are you going to come over here and sample one of my tea cakes?" Sarah Price glared at them in mock severity, her hands on her hips.

"Have a heart, Sarah." Adam groaned good-naturedly. "We just left Hester's booth. I don't think I could handle two cakes in one night."

"Lord love a duck, Adam!" The tiny woman looked aghast at his ignorance. "A tea cake's not a cake."

"It's not? But you called it—"

"A tea cake is a cookie, Adam," Tracy said, leaning close to speak over the gay chatter of a group of young girls.

"Then why is it called a cake?" he asked matter of factly.

"Because . . ." Tracy searched for an explanation even as she tried to hide her amusement. "It's always . . . uh . . . Because that's it's name, that's why." She put a definite end to the conversation.

"Since you've already spoiled yore appetite over at Hester's," Sarah said, "I'll just send some tea cakes with you. Stay right here and I'll put some in a poke." She scurried to the far end of her booth and rummaged among some papers.

"A poke?" Adam murmured quietly in Tracy's ear.

"A paper bag," she answered as quietly.

"Oh." He nodded. "Of course."

"Here now!" Sarah set the bulging bag before him. "Take these on home for later. I don't aim to toot my own horn, but Tracy can tell you that they're the best in the valley."

"Thanks, Sarah. I'm sure I'll enjoy them."

"I'm sure you will too," Sarah called immodestly after them as they moved back into the mainstream of the milling people. "Adam, be sure to have Tracy show you the special exhibit."

Adam and Tracy laughed and talked, exchanged greetings with friends as they walked, and Adam's hand again found Tracy's.

"I think this is the last," she said later as they stood before a table of delicate embroidery and crocheted doilies. A wizened old woman sat at the table, her eyes staring blankly at them. "Thank you, Opal, for sharing your work with us."

"Tracy?" A gnarled, brown-spotted hand searched toward the sound of her voice.

"Yes. It's Tracy." Young, firm fingers clasped the wrinkled and workworn hand.

"Let me see you. It's been months since you come to the house. Come down," the old woman urged. "Come down."

Quickly Tracy knelt before her. Opal's fingers stroked over her every feature, from her brow, across her eyes, to her cheeks and her lips. Finally they traced the path of the scar at her temple. "Have you kept well, little girl?"

"Very well, Opal."

"No more trouble with the words?"

"Not anymore."

"Good. Good." The gray head bobbed once. "Young man?"

"Yes, ma'am."

"Are you Tracy's man?"

"I . . ."

"Don't dillydally. Ain't no substitute for a straight answer. Either you are or you ain't."

Adam hesitated for a moment, his gaze traveling over the slender form of the kneeling woman. When he spoke, his voice was low and measured. "Yes, I think that perhaps I am."

"Think!" The old woman snorted. "The man who gets Tracy will know he's her man."

"Opal," Tracy interjected mildly, "Adam and I hardly know each other. We're just friends."

"Are you a friend, young man?" The milky white of the cataract-scarred eyes turned toward Adam.

"Yes."

It was only a single word, but Opal tilted her head, listening to its rich tone, savoring its intensity. She seemed to read in it what she wanted to know. Laying a steady hand on either side of Tracy's face, she kissed her forehead and smiled.

"Yore Adam is a good man, Tracy." She fondly patted Tracy's cheek. "Go now and have the fun you young'uns should instead of wasting time with a foolish old woman."

"Never foolish," Tracy murmured as she rose to her feet. "I'll be over to see you soon, Opal."

"You do that. I'd cherish it."

"It's a shame," Adam said as they walked away.

"What?" Tracy looked up at his frowning face.

"It's a shame that anyone who could do such beautiful work has to be handicapped and unable to continue."

Tracy smiled as they moved farther away. "It's a good thing Opal didn't hear that. She's the last person who would consider herself handicapped. Sure, she can't do the embroidery anymore, but she still crochets."

"How could she?" Astonishment was strong in Adam's words. "Some of those pieces were so delicate that they looked like cobwebs. How on earth could she do that when she's blind?"

"The patterns come from her memory and she says she sees with her fingers. I've watched her sit for hours crocheting, creating one lovely piece after another. If she could see, I doubt she would look down as she worked."

"The saddest part is that she can't see how beautiful they are."

"Yes," Tracy agreed, pleased that he understood.

"Couldn't something be done for her eyes?"

"There might have been in the past, but not now."

"With all the advances in medicine, I would think that there's some hope."

"No." Tracy shook her head sadly. "She's ninety-seven

years old and even frailer than she looks. I don't think she could survive any shocks to her system."

"Surely—"

"Adam." Tracy laid her hand on his arm in a gesture of comfort. "Opal would tell you not to fret yourself over her. She said long ago that she had made her peace with the blindness."

"She's a marvelous woman, isn't she?"

"We all think she is."

"These mountains seem to be good at producing magnificent women." Adam smiled and touched her hand. "Magnificent and beautiful."

"Flattery."

"Truth."

A glow suffused her face at his praise. "Do you think we should find Jed and Liza? They're going to think we deserted them."

"They don't need us. And anyway, we haven't seen that special exhibit Sarah told us about. Where is it?"

"It's over by the barn."

He turned to the booth in question. The laughter that lit his eyes faded and was replaced by wonder. "Tracy! What are these?"

Before she could answer, he moved closer to stand before a stunning array of miniature figures that had been carved from wood, then painted with a breathtaking realism. Beside each were the preliminary sketches and a watercolor that mirrored the final product.

"This is absolute genius! Whose work is it?" His hand hovered for an instant over the whimsical figure of a chipmunk curled sleepily on a leaf. "Are they for sale?"

"No."

"How can you be sure?"

"Because they're mine. Or at least they were."

"Yours?" Adam looked at her in surprise, and with the dawning of a new and even greater respect. "Why didn't you tell me? Why haven't I seen some of your work before? Surely you've shown it somewhere."

"Few of my carvings have ever been shown other than right here. These were gifts to my friends here in the valley. This display is their idea."

"You don't sell anything at all?"

"Only a piece of two when it was a necessity." Her finger stroked the colorful wing of a mallard duck, a decoy that had been a gift to Jed.

"It's strange, but I've seen something somewhere that reminds me of this." He looked down at a grouping of a fox and her three cubs tumbling in tall grass. "Tra . . . My God! You're *Trace*!"

"I do sign my work that way," she acknowledged.

"One of the loveliest things I've ever seen was in a small, exclusive gallery in New York. It was titled 'A Vixen at Play.' Even in miniature that fox was so realistic I waited for it to breathe. It carried the signature of Trace. Damn it, Tracy! What are you doing hiding yourself in these hills when you can do something this beautiful?"

"I like the mountains, Adam. They're my home; they always will be. I sketch, I paint, and I carve what I know and what I see around me. I do it for the pleasure it gives me. I never intended that it should be a career. My grandfather was the true artist in the family. If you know woodcarving, you probably know his name. He was called the Forest Walker."

"Of course," Adam muttered to himself. "I should have known." He looked at her as she stood illuminated by the dim light of the lanterns and the moonlight, and the last pieces of an old and unsolved puzzle fell into place. He said nothing, though, and waited for her to continue.

"Actually he started it as a sort of physical therapy for me. With the weaknesses left by my injuries, I could hardly hold the instruments and I cut myself more times than I care to remember. But he pushed and urged until I continued."

"It's a blessing that he did. But as a master carver himself, he would recognize your talent as unique."

Tracy's laugh was mirthless, tinged with the pain of remembered frustration. "You wouldn't say that if you could see my first efforts. Most were unrecognizable, shapeless masses, and often as not painted with my own blood."

"Yet in the face of it all, you never gave up." Adam wanted to take her into his arms, asking nothing but that she let him hold her.

"As my mind healed and I recovered more and more of my coordination, my skill grew. It became easier and easier, until one day I realized that I no longer needed the carving, but that I was doing it for the sheer love of it."

"Each of these has been a gift?"

"Yes." She picked up a lifelike figure of a plump piglet. "This was for Malcolm on his sixty-sixth birthday. The quail was for Bobby Toney. Raising quail was his 4-H project. The coon dog is Ezra's, the hummingbird, Sarah's. I have little I can give to my friends except my carvings, and they seem to appreciate them."

"How many pieces have you sold?"

"Only a few. The New York gallery you mentioned handled Grandfather's work, and they also seem willing to take mine."

"Gladly, I should think. Have they approached you about taking more pieces than you've offered?"

"I receive a letter from them with great regularity. I haven't bothered to open the last few. They all used to say the same thing. I suppose they still do."

"Why won't you listen to what they have to say?"

"Because I don't really want to sell anything. I'd rather give them to the people I know will enjoy them, not just sell to someone who's—who's a collector. And because I don't intend to leave here. This is my *home*."

"Hey, hey, it's all right." He curved his hand around the nape of her neck, drawing her near. "I didn't mean to push."

"I know." She rested her forehead against the muscled wall of his chest. "I'm sorry. I don't usually overreact like that. I guess I'm just tired."

"Would you like to go back to join Jed and Liza now? We could watch the dancers."

"I'd like that." She leaned her head back and smiled up at him as he released her.

"Tracy, Adam," Jed called to them, catching their attention as they neared the platform where a square dance was just ending. He was sitting with Liza, their blanket spread a bit apart from the others. "Come sit with us."

"You two made an evening of it just seeing the exhibits. Did you buy anything?" Liza asked Adam as he sat down and stretched out onto the grass.

"Didn't buy a thing. All I have to show for my study of the mountain crafts is this." He produced the bag of tea cakes. "Sarah made these. Would you like to share?"

"I'd love one. Maybe I could get her recipe." Liza blinked in confusion as all three burst into laughter.

"Now, what did I say that was so funny?" she demanded.

"Nothing, really, Liza." Adam wiped the grin from his face. "It's just that you're a city girl visiting the hills, and you sound like you were born here."

"Is there some law that says I can't enjoy cooking just because I happen to live in the city? You should know that I like to cook. You visit my apartment for dinner often enough."

"At your invitation," Adam reminded her. "If I didn't, you'd probably scour the bushes looking for someone to feed."

"You don't live with Adam and Summer?" Tracy

asked. She was sitting on the far side of the blanket, enjoying the teasing exchange between brother and sister.

"No," Liza said. "I would, but Adam won't hear to it. After Sharon died he insisted on hiring a housekeeper. If I hadn't forced myself on him, he wouldn't have let me come with them to the valley. I had a hard time convincing him that I wanted to see the mountain and that I love spending time with Summer."

"But you'd been ill," Adam protested.

"Adam." Liza looked at him in exasperation. "You know that it was only bronchitis and now I'm as good as new. In fact if you hadn't been so stubborn and hadn't insisted on that final doctor's appointment, I would have been here when—" She stopped short, realizing what she had been about to say. "Oh, Adam, I'm sorry."

"Never mind, Liza. I understand." He ruffled her tumbled curls and smiled.

"Liza," Jed said, stepping in to ease the awkward moment, "the band is back from their break and I'm sure they're going to be playing our song. Can you keep your foot out of your mouth long enough to dance?"

"I certainly hope so." She took his hand and let him help her to her feet as the first chords of the music began.

"C'mon. We're going to miss the first call," Jed said, virtually dragging her away.

"Poor Liza," Tracy murmured as she watched her join Jed in the intricate moves of the dance. "She didn't mean to bring up a painful subject."

"I know," Adam said. "She's a good kid, and whether she'll admit it or not, I couldn't have managed over the past two years without her. She's there when I need her."

"You're lucky to have her."

"Yes." Turning his gaze from Liza to Tracy, Adam was aware of Tracy's wistful look. "Are you sure you wouldn't like to dance?"

"I can't dance, Adam. I used to love it, but not anymore. My recovery has been almost total . . . except for the rhythm. Somehow I can't seem to get it right anymore."

It was a simple admission, but his memories of the vibrant young girl of years ago made it one that tore at his heart. He couldn't help but wonder if her calmness was a cover for her fear that she would make a mistake or that she would forget again. He suddenly realized why she had chosen such a lonely life.

"I'll be right back." In a quick move he was on his feet. He strode to the platform, weaving through the dancers to the leader of the band. The band leader didn't miss a beat as he listened to Adam and nodded his head. As quickly as he had gone, Adam was back by Tracy's side.

"Ladies and gentlemen," the leader announced over the loudspeaker. "We have an unusual request, but we agree that it's time for a change. So here it is, a nice, slow ballad. Here's your chance, fellas. With this one you can hold her close."

As the smooth beat of a gentle love song filled the air, Adam held out his hand to Tracy. "Tracy," he said.

"Adam, I can't."

"Yes, darling, you can."

"No."

"The music's slow, and I'll be with you."

She looked up into his eyes, wanting to take his hand but afraid.

"Come with me, Tracy. I need to hold you in my arms."

Suddenly, completely trusting, she did as he asked. He led her through the crowd to the dance floor. Once there, he waited a moment while she gathered her courage, then opened his arms. He breathed a soft sigh of relief when she stepped into them. Carefully, moving in short, slow steps, he led her through the dance.

At first uncomfortable and afraid, she held herself stiffly erect. Then with only a gentle pressure from his hand at her back, she moved closer until her head was nestled beneath his chin. Neither knew that the band played the song twice, nor that those around the dance floor were watching with silent pleasure.

As the final notes of the song faded away, it seemed natural that they should wander away, arm in arm, among the trees. They stopped by a brook that bubbled and sparkled in the bright moonlight.

"Tracy?" Adam threw an arm around her shoulders and drew her closer. His hard fingers tilted her head so that he could look into her eyes. As though in slow motion, he bent to kiss her. With a seeking hunger he parted her lips in the caress of a lover. He enfolded her body in his strong arms, pulling her hard against himself, letting her know his passion.

Tracy met his need with the fire he had kindled and gave herself up to enchantment. With a force of feeling that was new to her, she welcomed Adam's kiss with her own possessive caress. There was no shock, no outrage when his gentle fingers stroked the fullness of her breast. Nor did she protest when his hand cradled its weight, soothing the haughty nipple with his palm.

Adam groaned, a harsh and frustrated sound. He broke the kiss and dropped his hand. He molded her soft body to his own hard, taut one, resting his chin on her brow. His ragged breath stirred her hair.

"Who are you that you've become the center of my thoughts and my dreams?" he whispered. "Have you bewitched me, Tracy Walker?"

She stirred, then stepped away from his embrace. With her arms crossed, one hand resting at her throat, she stared over the water. "You've said it, Adam. I'm simply Tracy Walker. No more, no less. What I've done is nothing that any concerned human being wouldn't do for another. Be careful. What you feel now might be the result of your ordeal. Summer's safe and you're grateful. Maybe it's even a misguided sense of guilt over Wolfe."

"No! Summer *is* safe, and I'm more grateful than you

could ever know, but it has nothing to do with what I feel now."

"I'd like to believe that." She turned to face him, her eyes dark and secret in the shadows.

"You can, darling."

"No." She shook her head slowly. "It's too soon, our emotions are in a turmoil. We need to regain an even keel before we can know what we really feel for each other."

"Then will you come to Shadow? Will you spend some time there with me? Will you give me a chance to know you?"

"Yes. I'll come. For as long as you want me, or until we understand this attraction between us."

"I couldn't ask for any more than that . . . for now."

Five

"Is this where we'll be camped?"

"No such luck," Tracy said as she pulled supplies from the back of the jeep. "This is just an old logging trail. We have a bit of a walk ahead of us. None of it easy."

"Do you have a campsite chosen?"

She nodded as she shifted the frame of her heavily loaded pack. "We need to be near water and where there's a break in the underbrush. About midway up there's a small clearing that should serve our needs nicely. It has a stream that's more rock than anything else, but the water's clean and plentiful."

"Sounds good."

"The stream isn't very deep, and if you want to take a bath you have to sit on a rock in the middle. Even then the water would hardly come to your waist." Her laugh carried a far happier note than Adam had ever heard before. "But that should be more than enough, unless you enjoy frigid baths."

"I'm sure I can manage a quick dip no matter how icy, but since I don't relish the thought of a cold shave, I might use this as the excuse to grow the beard I've been considering."

"There is a small lake over on the other side of the

mountain that's fed by a hot spring, but it would be quite a walk."

"That sounds like it might be another of the unexplained oddities of Shadow."

"One of them," Tracy agreed, engrossed in checking her first aid kit one more time. She snapped it closed and turned. For a moment she stared at Adam, a half smile on her lips. "I wonder if it will be gray."

"What?"

"The beard."

"What beard?"

"The one you're going to grow."

"I was only teasing." He laughed as he shouldered his pack.

"I don't see why," she said as she did the same. "I think it would look most distinguished. Unless . . ." She gave him an impish grin and an enticing wink, then walked away.

"Hey! Wait." He rushed to catch up with her, sparing a quick look of admiration for her trim hips hugged so snugly by the heavy denim. "Don't leave me in suspense. When would my beard not be distinguished?"

"What beard?"

"The one I'm going to grow."

"Are you going to grow a beard, Adam?" She turned to look at him in mock surprise, a barely suppressed grin twitching her lips.

"Yes. A distinguished one, remember?" He was delighted as he fell willing prey to her quick tongue, loving the bright cheerfulness that lit her face.

"And maybe a red one."

"Red!" They had begun to move again, but now he stopped abruptly, an expression of absolute horror on his face. "A red beard?"

"Um-hm. The same color as Liza's hair. Gorgeous!"

"Gorgeous!" he choked on the word, watching Tracy as she climbed the slope, following a trail that was barely visible. As a low-hanging branch hid her from view, he started to chuckle, the sound quickly growing into a full, rolling laugh. "Where but on a crazy mountain like this would I find a woman who thinks I should grow a flaming red beard and calls it gorgeous?"

"Adam?" Her voice drifted back through the dense foliage of oak and evergreen. "Don't you think you look a bit silly standing by yourself on a mountainside talking when there's no one to listen except maybe a squirrel or a polecat or two?"

"Polecat as in skunk?"

"Would you quit stalling like a tenderfooted flatlander and come on?" Her voice was growing progressively distant. "I'm your leader, but I can't lead if you won't follow. Adam? Are you coming?"

"Coming, fearless leader. But I wonder if you'll be any more fearless than I if we do meet that polecat."

"Still talking to yourself, Adam?"

He gingerly pushed aside the prickly branch of a blackberry bush and found her waiting for him. She was leaning against a straight, skinny pine, her arms folded beneath her breasts, one foot crossed over the other. Dressed for the mountain and with her hair in its customary braid, she looked much as she had the first day he had seen her. Yet she was infinitely different.

Her aloof restraint had softened. A quiet spark of laughter and lightheartedness seemed to hover just beneath the surface. It had not been there when she had met him earlier that morning. She had been subdued and thoroughly efficient as she checked both his clothing and his equipment, from the high boots he wore at her insistence to the flashlight in his pack.

The change in her, slow and subtle yet clearly evident, was something to ponder. But for now he would simply appreciate it.

"Waiting for me, darling?" he said, teasing, giving her a slow, lingering look.

"Waiting and listening to you mutter."

"I was muttering, as you call it, to you."

"And what was it you were muttering to me?" She straightened from the tree, obviously enjoying the exchange.

"I was wondering if you would protect me with your wily woodsman's knowledge if we should meet with the aforementioned polecat."

"Sorry." She turned to continue up the trail. "If we meet one, you're on your own. I have a healthy respect for all wild animals, but the little creature in the striped suit strikes fear in the heart of any woodsman or woman, wily or otherwise."

"In other words, to put it bluntly, you'd run."

"Like a shot."

"Some leader you turned out to be."

"Wanna trade me in?" Climbing surefootedly, she didn't spare a glance in his direction.

"Not on your life."

"That's what I thought." This time her voice was softer, the hint of laughter gone. "Better save your breath, tenderfoot. The climb gets rough from here on."

"Yes'm." Adam applied himself to negotiating the twists and turns of the thorny, rock-cluttered path. It did, indeed, grow rougher and at times impassable. Agile and strong, a man used to strenuous and vigorous activity, he needed only to move with care. The pack on his back, heavy but well balanced, presented no problem, and his mind was free to roam to the woman ahead.

Tracy. She was an enigma, and Adam was intrigued by the multifaceted personality that was emerging. On the first day he had been struck by her cool competence and the studied confidence of every deliberate movement or word. She had met his anger with the understanding and kindness of a rare sensitivity. Then quietly, without fanfare or furor, she had traded one life for another.

He had shared with her the grieving for a loyal friend, Wolfe. And a lost friend, Sharon. In the deep of the night, buffeted and racked by loss, she had slept trustingly in his arms, only to disappear as quickly as she had come.

Tracy. She was a woman of many moods. He had been burned by the fire of her temper and cut by her truthful tongue. He had felt her kinship with his motherless child and watched her loving patience with the blind Opal. He had learned of her talent and her generosity with her carvings. And he had seen her fear.

When he had led her onto the dance floor the night before, he had also gained her trust. In the face of overwhelming self-doubt she had given herself into his care. It was a step toward the future, sealed by the kiss they had shared beside the brook.

Adam had no illusions that the way to his goal would be without its problems. Watching her that morning, seeing her mood lighten, he had been astounded by the effect the mountain had on her. At first he had doubted the strange thought that had begun to form in his mind. But now he believed. In some way Shadow was her confidence. Here she knew peace. For the first time he began to understand the strength of the hold Shadow had on her. A frown crossed his face. He nodded once slowly, then moved forward again.

At one point the terrain flattened into a small plateau before rising again. The trees nearer the crest had grown more stunted and sparse, offering a view of the gentle peaks of the flanking mountains.

"This is beautiful," Adam said as he stood by Tracy, gazing out at the panorama before him. For as far as the eye could see, rolling tree-covered lands stretched toward the horizon. "I don't see the valley and the village."

"We're on the far side of the mountain. The valleys to the east were never settled."

"Then we've been climbing around as we've climbed up."

"Right. The logging camp was about halfway up. That

was where we left the jeep. The path we took was used by the loggers as they came up from the sawmill."

"What did they log? This wood doesn't look like it would be worth the effort."

"It wasn't."

"Is that why the trail is so faint? It was never traveled much?"

"It was hardly used at all. Shadow didn't want them here. For every tree that was cut down, a man died."

Adam turned to her, shocked by the conviction in her voice. "You don't believe that."

"In the days before automation, logging was slower and harder. More men were needed. Nine trees were cut; nine men died. Finally no one would work here. The business ended before it was started. None of the trees cut were ever taken completely away from Shadow. The project was abandoned before they could be."

"Is that the basis for a legend?"

"Yes. The old-timers say that if you listen carefully, you can hear the sound of the axes. There's no sound in the world quite like that of wood being chopped."

"The axes are supposed to belong to the dead men, I suppose."

"They spend eternity cutting trees that never fall."

"Have you heard them?"

"Yes." She turned her back on the scene, facing the starkness of the mountain. "We'll be camping just beyond that patch of woods. There's a clearing there and the stream I told you about."

Adam rapidly took some pictures of the plateau for his book. The loggers and the faint trail that remained would be of interest to his publisher. Surreptitiously he also shot two photographs of Tracy. After replacing the lens cover, he put the camera away and shouldered his pack again. "Ready."

Tracy moved from the sunlight into the shade of the dark pines. Brambles and briars were thick on the ground, but a narrow path cut cleanly through them.

Adam was startled when, without warning, they entered a tiny clearing.

The land was perfectly flat. Grass, lush and green, carpeted the meadow. A wide but shallow and slow-moving brook wound and looped among the scattered trees. There was none of the raw starkness of the rest of the mountain that Adam had seen, and it didn't fit his image of Shadow.

"We'll cross the brook," Tracy said. "The best campsite is on the other side." She led him to the bank and they looked down at the sparkling water.

"Boy! You weren't kidding when you said this would be mostly rocks." Adam laughed as he surveyed the piles and clusters of smooth gray granite stones. "There's not a sharp edge here."

"Over the years the water has tumbled them about, wearing their edges smooth. There are rocks all along this stream, but for some reason more seem to have accumulated here."

"A legend?"

"None that I know of. It's just Rocky Creek. There's no significance to the rocks or the name, appropriate though it is." Tracy slipped free of her pack. "Let's cross and find the best spot to set up camp first. Then we can take our supplies over. We might decide that this would be best. I haven't been here in a while, and things do change in the mountains."

Adam gratefully shrugged off his own pack and flexed his shoulders. Feeling more cramped than tired, he stretched and muffled a yawn.

"Sleepy?" Tracy asked. "It's the altitude. It affects some people that way."

"I'm accustomed to the altitude," Adam contradicted her. "It's lack of sleep. I lay awake into the small hours of the morning thinking of you. Remembering how you felt in my arms as we danced, and how your lips trembled when I kissed you. Did you sleep well, Tracy?"

"I slept like the proverbial log," she lied, feeling his

gaze on her lips, recalling the power of his kiss. She turned away abruptly. "We'd better decide on a campsite soon. Sunset comes with little warning up here. I'd like to get set up and gather firewood while there's still light. It's safer that way."

"Rattlesnakes?"

"Among other things."

He lifted a quizzical eyebrow. "Such as?"

"Bears, mountain lions, raccoons, deer. Shall I go on?"

"I'll worry about the snakes and the bears and the lions, but why the raccoon and the deer?"

"They wouldn't hurt us, but both the 'coon and the deer are notorious for foraging in camping supplies. So are the lion and bear for that matter."

"Then we set up camp, do our chores, finish with our supplies, and before we turn in for the night we hang anything interesting by a rope from a high tree limb. Right?"

"You've got it. But let me warn you, an enterprising 'coon wouldn't be defeated by that." Tracy laughed. "Hopefully, one that hungry or just that curious won't find us."

Adam checked his watch, then looked at the sky, which had begun to darken. "If we plan to get all that done before nightfall, we need to get started, don't we?"

"Right. Maybe you'd better wait here while I go over to check the old campsite to make sure that it's safe. Rest a minute."

Tracy stepped carefully onto one of the many rocks that lay partially submerged in the crystal-clear stream. Scattered randomly through the water like hundreds of steppingstones, they formed a natural path to the opposite side. She was halfway across when Adam spoke.

"There's no need for me to sit here doing nothing. I'll come too.

"Adam. Wait!" She was turning around as she spoke. "These rocks are—"

Splash!

"—slippery."

Her last word was little more than a gasp. The water that showered over her head and shoulders was so frigid that she lost her breath. For an instant her lashes were weighted by the fine spray and she couldn't see. When she blinked the moisture away she was greeted by the spectacle of Adam sitting waist-deep in the swirling water.

He sat calmly, with one arm leaning against his bent knee. His face was blank, registering neither shock nor outrage. From his unruffled manner, one could almost believe that to be sitting fully clothed in an icy mountain stream was a common occurrence for him.

"Are you hurt, Adam?"

"No."

"Are you sure?"

"Positive."

"Then, I have to tell you"—she choked slightly on the words and her lips refused to obey her efforts at keeping a solemn expression—"that was the poorest imitation of a windmill I've ever seen."

"You think so, huh?" Adam still didn't move.

Her battle was lost. From only a hint of a grin, to a muffled chuckle, the laughter rose in her until it flowed over him. A happy laugh, a carefree laugh, and she was again the young, exciting Tracy of years ago.

Charmed by the lightning-swift transformation, he sat transfixed. His only reaction to her amusement was a good-natured grin. He didn't want to move, afraid that if he did, the moment would be lost.

"Oh, Adam." Her laughter rose and fell with each new breath. "You are truly an amazing man."

"I am?"

"Yes, indeed."

"How so?"

"No one else could carry this off with such dignity. The sitting, not the falling." Her merriment at last subsided, only to erupt again in a fit of giggles at the memory of his flailing arms and flying legs. She fought to regain her composure, then, striving for a serious tone, spoke with exaggerated gravity. "You do know that you'll be very uncomfortable if you don't change soon?"

"I know."

"You did bring a change of clothes, didn't you?"

"As instructed." He nodded but made no attempt to rise.

Tracy stepped carefully onto the rock that had been Adam's downfall and leaned over to offer him her hand. A puzzled look crossed her face as his gaze moved over her and his expression altered subtly. Still, he did not move, nor did he accept her help.

"Adam." She rested her hands on her hips and looked down at him sternly. "Are you going to sit there all day?"

"I might."

His tone was level, almost casual, but there was something in his eyes. A spark of hidden excitement? Tracy wondered, even more perplexed.

"Aren't you cold?"

"I really hadn't given it much thought." He looked down at the water as if just becoming aware of it. "I've been too busy admiring the view to pay it much attention."

"Oh, dear." Tracy's words were a low moan of realization. In her first concern that he might be hurt, then in the midst of her hilarity, she had given no thought to herself.

She had dressed that morning as always when climbing Shadow. Her clothing had to be durable, but also comfortable. A rough fabric that chafed or rubbed could become agony on the trail. Her heavy cotton shirt was both thick and soft and afforded the greatest protection, except when it was drenched. Now it molded and clung to her, leaving no doubt that she had forgone one article of clothing—the one that could cause her untold misery when she carried a heavy pack.

Tracy knew that Adam saw, beyond a doubt, that beneath her blouse she wore nothing.

"I—I'm sorry" she stammered, flustered by his stare. "It's just that with the heavy . . ." She stopped as his gaze again traveled over her.

"Don't apologize to me." His smile caressed her, deepening her embarrassment when she realized she had made no effort to turn away. "Seeing you like this makes falling in the creek worthwhile."

Something in his voice took her breath away as surely and as sharply as the cold water had. She turned and hurried heedlessly across the stones. "I'll check that site now. You can change while I'm gone."

When she reached the other side, Adam rose from the water, watching her as she walked through a patch of knee-high grass.

"Are you frightened, Tracy?" he murmured. "Or only confused?" Not until she had moved out of sight did he wade back to the bank to change and wait.

Tracy spent longer than she had intended in surveying the campsite, and finally ended up at a small tributary of the stream. As she tossed stones into the rippling water, her mind was filled with conflicting thoughts. She was at once disturbed by the unwitting display of her body and pleased that Adam had found her desirable.

She was astonished by the strength of her own surging response and wondered if she could cope with an attraction so powerful. After her words of caution the night before, she was dismayed to find his teasing on a sunlit day created the same tantalizing excitement as an intimate caress in the moonlight.

Trying to untangle her turbulent thoughts, she asked herself the inevitable questions. What part in her limited life was Adam destined to play? What of herself could she give to him and survive?

He was a virile man, one who had perhaps known many women, and had loved one deeply. A woman's body held no mysteries for him and yet . . . what was it about the way he looked at her? What was it she saw in his eyes?

In the peace of the meadow she searched in vain for answers. Only when dusk began to fall rapidly did she turn back to the stream. By the time she had recrossed the path of stones, her shirt had dried enough to restore her modesty. Tracy wished ruefully that her sense of perspective could be restored as easily.

When she stepped on shore, she saw that Adam had dressed. He was lounging against a large boulder, his face upturned to the waning light, his eyes closed. Nothing about him moved but the blade of grass between his lips.

Walking with her naturally quiet step, she had a precious moment to observe him. With a sudden clarity that brought the serenity that had eluded her, she realized that the answer to her questions lay in the future. She must for now simply accept what each day might bring.

"Are you all right?" His quiet words broke into her thoughts. Lost in them, she hadn't been aware that he had opened his eyes.

"What?"

"Are you all right?" he repeated as gently, his gaze filled with tender concern.

"I'm fine, Adam."

"Then hadn't we better make camp?"

"Yes." She forcibly drew in her wandering thoughts. "It will be dark soon. We'd better get a move on."

"Where to?"

"The other side." She tilted her head in mock earnestness. "That is, *if* you think you can make it."

"You just lead the way, darlin'," he drawled. "I'll be right behind you, taking every step you do."

"Good enough. Shall we?" She hefted her pack onto her shoulders, waited until he had adjusted his own, then, carefully picking her path, led him over the slick stones.

Darkness has fallen over the mountain by the time their camp had been set up and supper done. Adam had hoisted the remaining foodstuffs over a tree limb while Tracy washed the last of their dishes in the creek.

He was sitting before the fire as she tucked them away in her pack. "Doesn't it bother you?"

"What?" On her knees by the pack, she paused to look up at him.

"There's just the two of us here. The valley's a small community. Won't there be talk?"

"Why should there be?" She finished in one quick move, then sat down by the fire and looked into the flames. "I'm a guide and a tracker, simply doing my job. I've been alone in the company of men many times. As far as I know, no one's ever said anything. But"—she shrugged—"it wouldn't matter if they did."

"The liberated woman?"

"If doing what I enjoy to the best of my ability regardless of my sex means that I'm liberated, then yes, I suppose I am," she said, not looking away from the dancing fire.

"Do you act as a guide often?"

"If I like the person or the party, and if I'm not involved in something else."

He frowned at the thought of the possible danger in which this could put her. "How can you judge whether or not someone is trustworthy?"

"Mostly instinct."

"Then you're never afraid, not even of the mountain."

"I love this mountain. There's nothing evil here. She just demands more respect than the foolhardy realize."

"She?"

"Yes, Shadow's a woman," she murmured more to

herself than to Adam. Silence stretched between them again, but it was not uncomfortable.

A night bird called; a mountain lion screamed in the distance. Adam stirred and leaned toward the fire. "There's about one more cup of coffee left. Would you like to share it?"

"Yes, I would." She watched his strong profile silhouetted by the flames as he filled their cups and set the pot aside. Short dark hairs glistened on his wrist as he handed the cup to her. Their fingers brushed as she took it from him. Her free hand clasped his, turning it over to look at the callused palm. "A rugged hand for a photographer. You're very strong, Adam."

He turned his hand over to twine his fingers with hers and took a sip of coffee. "My photography takes me many places. I learned very early in my career that studio work was not for me. I suppose I'm a bit of a hunter, but my weapon is my camera. I have to be fit to go the places I do."

"Tell me about your work." Tracy was contented as she had never been before, simply sitting beneath Shadow's summit with Adam's hand warm and strong over hers.

"Mostly I've done adventure series, things like rafting down white water. I've been in the desert and the rain forest. Once I photographed an erupting volcano. Another time I flew with a hurricane-watch crew. Those were fantastic pictures that have been compiled into a book. Shadow will be a feature in my next one. It'll deal with strange and beautiful phenomena of America. I'll take the pictures, then write a short text on each."

"It sounds exciting."

"It has been."

"You've traveled a great deal and to some interesting places."

"Umm." He paused, then answered her unasked question. "Sharon traveled with me most of the time. If she couldn't go on the actual location, she stayed nearby. We were never apart for more than a few weeks, if that much."

"What did you do after Summer was born?"

"For a while I didn't take any long-range assignments. Later, she stayed with Sharon's mother. She still does if I have to be away for a time. I try to keep my absences short. As an only parent, I feel it's imperative that I spend as much time as possible with her. But I don't know what I would have done without Marjorie. She loves being a grandmother and she's been a life saver."

"Liza said you had a housekeeper."

"I do. Cora takes care of the house and the shopping. She watches Summer after school and on the weekends some. But when I'm away for long, I want a member of the family with her. It's important that she feel a sense of security."

"Security is a very necessary thing. She'll be the stronger for it." Tracy said no more as she tossed away the last of her coffee, then sat mesmerized by the dying fire.

Adam wondered if, perhaps, she spoke of a frightened young woman whose speech and memory had been impaired, and who had found her security on Shadow. He tightened his hold on her hand. "It's been a long day. Do you think we should build the fire up a bit, then turn in?"

"I am tired. I didn't know how much until now. I'll spread out the sleeping bags while you add the wood."

The crackle of the burning limbs, the faint smell of wood smoke that drifted on the breeze, and the welcome comfort of the soft sleeping bags slowly lulled them to sleep. Tracy had laid their bags on either side of the fire. After the climb they had welcomed the rest for their tired bodies, and a whispered good night was hardly finished or hardly heard as heavy lids closed with fatigue.

A soft, happy sound filled the meadow, floating like

the smoke on the playful breeze that still teased the leaves of the trees. It trilled through the air again, starting low, then rising to a gay, bell-like note. Adam bolted upright, pushing his sleeping bag aside.

"What was that?"

"Umm?" Tracy turned toward him.

"There must be a raccoon into our food. I heard him chatter." He looked up at the swaying bundle of their supplies. Nothing had disturbed it. There was no sign that anything had been near. "I must have scared it away."

"I don't think so. I mean, I don't think it was a 'coon. It was probably Alice."

"Who's Alice?"

"We'll know for sure in the morning if it was her. Good night, Adam." She pulled the cover up under her chin. Soon her even breathing told him that she had again drifted to sleep.

He sat as he was for quite some time. He scanned the trees and the clearing about them. There was nothing there. At last he lay back down, settling himself comfortably for the night. "Good night, my darling Tracy," he whispered. "And good night, Alice . . . whoever you are."

In a matter of seconds his breathing matched Tracy's. The stream babbled its way down the mountain. A rabbit feasted on the succulent grass, an owl hooted, a whippoorwill called. The bright flame of the fire sank to the red-gray hue of dying embers.

Somewhere far in the forest a sound rose and fell like the giggle of a happy child.

Six

The tantalizing aroma of coffee and bacon teased his nostrils. Adam woke slowly, not abruptly nor startled, but with an instant awareness of time and place. Rolling to his side, he watched Tracy as she tended the fire and the heavy pans that rested on the rack above it. By the frying pan a small pot gave off a cloud of steam.

Adam was completely captivated by her fresh loveliness, and by the memory of how she had looked the night before—like an Indian woman who saw to the needs of her mate. The thought that he might belong to her was infinitely satisfying. He stretched leisurely, folded his hands beneath his head, and allowed himself the luxury of listening, feeling, and appreciating.

"If you want this while it's at least edible, you'd better crawl out and hop to," Tracy called suddenly.

"Hop to?"

"It means, simply, that you'd better get busy, buster."

"Yes'm." Adam slipped from the sleeping bag, chuckling at the colorful idioms of the local speech.

Naked to the waist and on bare feet, he dashed to the stream and splashed water over his face and hands. Tracy watched him kneeling there with water gleaming like jewels in his hair and on his skin. Not one brisk move nor shivering breath escaped her rapt attention.

As he began to rise she quickly turned away and busied herself with the fire.

When he returned and huddled before its warmth, she was already dishing up the eggs she had scrambled. After he had shrugged into his shirt, she handed him the plate and cup.

"This looks terrific," he said eagerly. "I can't remember when I've been so hungry. What's in the pot on the fire?"

"Water for you to shave."

"Ah, then you've decided against my beard?"

"On the contrary," she said. "I think you would be quite handsome in it, even if it were red. I put the water on in case you decided you wanted it."

He rubbed his hand across his chin, grinning at the roughness. If it was a beard she wanted, she would get one. "Then for now I think I'll forgo the shave."

"Good." She deftly lifted the pot and tipped the steaming water over the campfire. "This should be completely cold by the time we're ready to move out."

This time Adam did the dishes in the creek while Tracy packed away their sleeping bags. These, too, were put out of the way of any curious roaming animals. They would spend the day ranging over the mountain, with Tracy showing Adam the interesting points of Shadow. Before nightfall they would return to this base camp. Though neither mentioned it, they each looked forward to being unencumbered by the weight of packs.

"That's the last of them. My dishpan hands and I are ready to go whenever you are."

"You don't make it a practice of doing dishes, I assume." Tracy grinned at him, eyeing his fingers, which were red from the cold water.

"That's what I have a housekeeper for at home. But in my work and in the wilds I've done my share."

"And quite well," she said, thinking how comfortably he had adjusted to the trek up the mountain.

"Thank you, my sweet. I do try." He bowed low in exaggerated servility that the wicked glint in his eyes belied.

"If you're really ready, what we had better try is to get started with this little jaunt. We have a lot of territory to cover today."

"Before we go, aren't you going to tell me about the sound we heard last night?"

"Alice was playing in the meadow. What we heard was her laughter."

"How can you tell and who the devil is Alice?"

"I'll show you on the way out of camp. But first, do you have what you need?" Tracy studied him carefully. The attire of a mountain man suited him well, enhancing his already rugged masculinity. As she appreciated Adam the man, she realized that only a fool would doubt his virile appeal. Her gaze slowly traced the long, lean lines of his body, then came to rest on his face.

His skin had grown darker in his days in the valley. When he smiled at her as he did now, he was a man of irresistible charm.

The promised beard was only a stubble of no discernible color. Tracy laughed aloud as she remembered his horror that it might be red. The sound broke her trance, and she became acutely aware that she had been staring at Adam.

Giving herself a mental shake and wondering why she found the sight of him so seductive, she forced her thoughts to the moment. "Do you have your knife and your canteen?"

"Both." For emphasis, he shook the canvas-covered canteen and his left hand came to rest on the hilt of the knife at his belt.

"Good. I have the first aid kit and some chocolate bars."

"What about lunch?"

She laughed again at his worried expression. "Hungry already, Adam?"

"After a morning of hiking in this rarefied atmosphere, I'm sure to be, and soon. If I grow faint from hunger, will you comfort me, darlin'?" The teasing in his voice did not reach his eyes.

Tracy quickly turned away for fear that he would read her thoughts in her face. Though she must speak of practical things, her mind was creating images of Adam, hard and strong, held against her breasts . . . but in desire rather than comfort.

"Don't worry." She fought to subdue a startling quiver of anticipation. "I won't let you starve. We should be back here by lunch. If not, the candy should suffice."

"Too bad. Suddenly, starving begins to have its merits. I was hoping to get your arms around me with less drastic measures, but . . ."

"Idiot!" Tracy smiled, glad for his lighthearted changing of the mood, his banishing of the serious note that seemed to lie beneath every flip comment. "If you've quite finished with your foolishness, we'd better move on, or we won't make it back by lunch."

She kicked at the dead fire with the toe of her boot. Once assured that there was no danger of a spark igniting, she faced him. "Shall we go, Adam?"

He followed her, observing that she also wore a sheathed knife at her waist, as she had the day before. When she wasn't wearing it, it was never far from her reach. Here on Shadow it seemed to have become an essential part of her. He wondered why.

"Careful," Tracy warned. "The rocks will be even slicker from the dew. Step exactly where I do. When we get to the other side, I have something pretty to show you. Ready?"

At his nod she stepped onto the low, flat rocks, picking her path very slowly and with meticulous care. Adam did as she had instructed, not relishing the thought of another dunking in the icy water. Precisely fitting his footsteps to hers, he joined her where she waited on the opposite shore.

She touched his arm lightly. "Look, Adam."

His gaze followed the direction her gesture indicated. The meadow was filled with clumps of tiny flowers, their purple and yellow petals drenched with shimmering dewdrops. There were hundreds of the small clumps clustered closely together.

Tracy had been guilty of understatement when she had called it pretty. The flower-strewn meadow was breathtaking, Adam mused.

"Beautiful," he murmured. "I've never seen anything like it. What are they?"

Tracy smiled, pleased that he found pleasure in something of Shadow. "These are Alice's flowers. They bloom in the foothills in the spring and some people call them Johnny-Jump-ups. But to those of us who live in the valley, they've always been Alice's flowers."

"Why?"

"Many years ago a small child lived at the base of the mountain. These were her favorite flowers. She would spend hours gathering them, then she wove them into chains to make bracelets and crowns.

"On an early spring day she was on Shadow gathering them when a terrible storm rose. There was thunder and lightning and a strong wind. Trees were blown over and small landslides obliterated the paths. Alice was lost."

She looked away from the multitude of flowers, wanting to see Adam's face as she finished the legend. "The mother was inconsolable, for Alice was her last surviving child. The old-timers say that they thought she would die from grief. Then one day as she wandered the paths her little girl had loved, she heard the laughter and saw the flowers, and her hurt was eased. Shadow had shown her that the child was happy here among the flowers. Everywhere Alice goes they appear, no matter what time of year."

To Adam, it was a beautiful story told by an even more beautiful voice. He knew Tracy wanted him to believe, but his practical mind could not accept the legend. As he adjusted his camera, he offered his logical argument.

"The temperatures we had last night were more like spring than summer or fall. That must have stimulated their growth out of season."

"Don't you see that the flowers are growing exactly where a small child's footsteps would fall?" It was her only hope of disputing his reasoning.

"Only a random pattern. Coincidental." Taking picture after picture of the flowers, he failed to see the flash of disappointment that crossed her face.

Tracy remained silent, waiting until he had taken all the shots he wanted. Why, she wondered, was it so important that he see Shadow as she did? Why did she need him to understand that Alice's flowers had been a gift of kindness? For this man to feel as she did about the mountain meant far more to her than anything had in a long time. But perhaps it was too soon. She offered herself this straw of hope.

When he put his camera away she moved silently on through the clearing. Careful not to crush the tiny, violetlike flowers, she led him to the path that would take them higher onto the peak.

It wasn't long before the gradual slope of the trail grew steeper and, at times, nearly impassable. There could be little doubt that few came here. Adam's muscles began to ache from the sharp incline, but Tracy showed no sign of tiring. Her pace was as steady as it had been at the first. She seemed to draw strength from the mountain, its ruggedness no obstacle.

The sun bore down on them intermittently as it broke through the rustling leaves of oak and poplar. At a point where the path widened, a small patch of color caught Adam's attention and he paused in his climbing.

"Tracy." His voice was low, but she heard him and turned back.

He was kneeling at the edge of the trail, his hands half hidden in the tall grass. She couldn't see what he was doing and took a step toward him. When he rose he was holding a flower, and he quickly walked over to her. Even standing on the downward slope he had to bend to her.

"Alice has been here too," he said. With deliberate care he slipped his fingers under the V of her blouse, then threaded the fragile stem of the flower through the buttonhole. The backs of his fingers brushed her bare skin, resting for a moment in the cleft between her breasts.

Intent on his task he bent nearer, his warm breath caressing her. Tracy wondered if he knew that he was touching her or if he was feeling any of the unfamiliar sensations that were exploding within her. Surely he could sense how feverish she had become and that her heart was racing like mad beneath his hand, leaving her drained of any will of her own.

When she thought she could stand no more, he finished his task and moved away, slipping his fingers slowly from within her blouse. Freed from his touch, her body was again hers to command.

Totally oblivious of his overwhelming effect on her, Adam looked down into eyes that had grown even blacker as she looked up at him in question. In innocence he misinterpreted her expression.

"It's a beautiful flower and a beautiful story. One doesn't have to believe the legend to appreciate it. I like Alice. She reminds me of you, for you both love Shadow." He smoothed a loose tendril of hair back from Tracy's face, then brushed her lips lightly with his. "Now, what's on the agenda of mysteries for the day?"

Shaken to the very essence of her soul by his inadvertent touch and light kiss, Tracy couldn't gather her wits. No thoughts, serene or deliberate, were forthcoming.

She was caught in a web of awakening desire that had little to do with reason or logic.

This wasn't the dark, despairing forgetfulness of the past, but speechless delight. The panic that lurked behind every forgotten word had no place amid what Adam offered. The sight of him was pleasing. His voice was soothing. His kiss was magic and his hands on her body brought enchantment. But now he only smiled down at her.

You were going to accept serenely what each day brought, she chided herself in that part of her mind that still functioned rationally.

"Tracy, darlin'." Adam touched her cheek with the back of his hand. "If you keep looking at me like you did at the dance, I might think you've begun to fall in love with me." His hand closed gently about her chin, then moved down to circle her neck. His arm rested against her full breasts. In a voice hoarse with hope, he whispered, "Have you, sweet Tracy? Do you love me?"

"I don't know." The words were low, murmured through trembling lips.

"Could it just be that here on Shadow you're more relaxed and your guard is down?"

"I've been on Shadow with men before. Many times." Though she offered no explanation, Adam knew that it had never before been like this.

He was almost certain that this Tracy did care for him. But once they left Shadow, would she grow aloof and distant? Would she again cloak her uncertainties in that calm deliberation that made her unapproachable? She had friends in the valley, friends who loved her, but no one truly knew her. Not Jed, nor Sarah and Ezra. Not the amazing Opal, nor even himself. But he would, he vowed. Somewhere in the reconciliation of the two Tracys he would find the whole woman.

And she would be his. He respected the mystique of the mountain even as he rejected it and knew he must go cautiously. What might be his for the taking could be lost, should he move too soon. He must have all of her—both the valley's Tracy and Shadow's Tracy.

A squirrel, impatient that they should move on, chattered fiercely and a smile lightened Tracy's face as she turned toward him. Adam chuckled at the almost comic figure that was glaring down at them from the gnarled limb of a tree.

"If I looked silly standing by myself yesterday, then the two of us must be a riot," he said. "Do you think that little fellow thinks we're crazy?"

"Undoubtedly," Tracy said. "We could be standing too near his cache of winter nuts. Something's making him distinctively nervous. Anyway, we should move on if we're to stay on schedule."

"Not just yet." Adam drew her to him. Holding her thus, he felt as if some part of himself—one that he had not known existed—had come home. No matter that he teased about standing so long and so still on the lonely trail, it seemed very right to hold her here on the face of Shadow.

Stroking her sleek hair, he looked up at the crest of the mountain barely visible through the leaves. Its hold on Tracy was strong and far-reaching. It was as a moving force in the life of this woman, whom Adam now realized he loved passionately and unendingly. As he stared at the bleak, rocky face of the peak, Adam mentally issued a challenge. *I must woo her from you, old woman. I must do it slowly and with infinite care. . . . but I will win.*

The squirrel chattered stridently and Adam put Tracy from him. "I think we'd better move on before the little fellow attacks us."

"You needn't worry. The natives are friendly."

"Tracy! Wait." He caught her hand as she had turned to continue up the trail. "Neither of us are fools. We both know that something powerful is happening between us. If we're careful and move cautiously, it could become a beautiful thing. But right now it's so explosive, the wrong move, the wrong word, could destroy it. Let's leave it for a while. Let it sit in the back of our minds and our hearts until we understand it better."

She stared directly into his serious eyes. "How do we come to understand it, Adam? And how do we keep it in the background?"

"We learn to understand it, whatever *it* is, by learning about each other. We keep it in the background by strength of will, and let's hope I have the discipline to do it."

"You can. You're a strong man, Adam."

"Not where you're concerned, Tracy. It won't be true strength that will keep me from you, but fear. I'm afraid I'll lose you before you're ever really mine."

"Then we must be very careful, mustn't we?"

"You do know, don't you, Tracy, that the real decision rests with you?"

"Yes. I know."

For the remainder of their climb their resolution was not mentioned again. While the sights and the tales of Shadow might have been uppermost in their minds, thoughts of their relationship, and what it might become, were never far away.

As they neared the top, Tracy veered onto a less evident trail, pushing her way through dense, unbending undergrowth. Suddenly the brush gave way to a clearer but still rugged path that led straight to the mouth of a cave. Mounds of dirt and loose rocks nearly obscured its entrance.

"Wait here while I check to be sure the cave isn't inhabited," Tracy said. "I'd rather not blunder in on a bear or a wildcat, or even a rattlesnake that might have set up residence since I was here last."

"I'll go with you," Adam said instantly.

"No!" Tracy was adamant. "If I need to move fast, I'd rather not have to worry about anyone but myself."

"Damn it, Tracy. If there's a chance you might be in danger, I should be with you."

"Please." She touched his hand lightly. "I'm accustomed to doing this sort of thing. You aren't. I couldn't bear it if I let you go in there and you were hurt."

"Then we'll skip it. I can get enough material for my book without risking that you might be harmed."

"No. I want you to see this. If you don't, the whole climb will have been for nothing. I've been in this cave many times, Adam. I'll be careful."

Tracy turned away, allowing him no chance to argue further. She agilely scaled the rocks, slipping only once as the dirt shifted under her weight. Before he could call out, she disappeared into the yawning blackness of the cave.

For what seemed like an eternity, Adam waited. The day was not hot, but drops of perspiration beaded on his forehead. Twice he looked at his watch. The hands had barely moved, but he would have sworn that an hour had passed. With his camera still slung over his shoulder, he paced back and forth before the gaping hole. With each step his worry grew until he was near panic.

Abruptly he turned. He had one foot on the mound of debris, meaning to go after her, when Tracy stepped from the darkness into the light.

"My God, darling! Are you all right? You were gone for so long, I was afraid you might be hurt."

"Adam." Her hand on his arm eased his agitation a bit. "You can see for yourself I'm perfectly fine. It's a fairly deep cave. It took me a while to check it out. I'm sorry. I didn't mean to worry you."

"I was coming in after you." Hearing the hoarse strain in his voice, she knew he was still far from calm.

"There was no need." She leaned forward to brush a pine needle from his hair. "There was truly no danger," she said softly, soothingly, "but I'm glad you cared."

Her fingers in his hair rekindled the very thing Adam had sworn to himself he would control. He wanted to snatch her from that pile of ugly dirt and draw her close against himself, to protect her from any harm. Instead, with fists clenched and teeth gritted, he willed his mind to accept.

This was Tracy's territory. She had lived here for many years. She knew the vagaries of Shadow. In truth, she was probably far safer here than anyone else would be. Still, he couldn't repress the insidious thought that in some way Shadow would take her from him. Adam knew he was being irrational, but his clear, orderly mind was helpless before this malignant fear.

"Tracy," he said finally, "I never meant to doubt your skill. I do understand that you know what you're doing. It's just that—"

"Hush, Adam." She laid a hand across his lips. "I know. Now, come with me." Lacing her fingers through his, she drew him up and over the mound, then into the cave.

By the time they had taken only a few steps they were engulfed in a pitch-black darkness that was totally unrelieved by any spark of light. Until his eyes adjusted from the brightness of day to the dark void, he could only follow where Tracy led. She moved carefully but easily through the cave.

"How the devil can you see?"

"I can't," she replied with a laugh. "I'm relying on memory."

"Do you mean to tell me that you came into this utter darkness not knowing what you might find, and you couldn't see?" Adam was quickly and fearfully angry at what he considered to be a foolish risk.

"No, Adam," Tracy said reasonably. "I had a flashlight."

"Then why on earth aren't we using it now?"

"Because I want the cave to be a surprise. Stop. Stay here for a second and close your eyes."

"Close my eyes in this? Whatever for? I can't see anything with them open."

"Please? Just do as I ask."

"Okay. If you insist, but what surprise could a cave hold?"

"You'll see. Are they closed?"

"As requested." Adam grinned in the darkness, thinking that she sounded much as Summer did when she shared a pretty rock or a wildflower with him.

"Don't move. I'll be right back."

Adam obeyed. He heard the soft sound of her step growing gradually fainter. Twice he heard the chink of glass bumping against something and twice he heard the rasp of a match being struck. There was nothing more until Tracy spoke from nearby.

"You can open your eyes now."

The sight that greeted him was astonishing. The sounds he had heard were the matches lighting two oil lamps. Their pale glow lit what appeared to be a small, comfortable room. The walls were dry and hung with intricate needlepoint designs. Handmade furniture that had been cut and fitted precisely, then rubbed and polished to a rich patina, was scattered about. Cushions of a heavy material were tied to the seats of the chair. Small, bright pillows added a splash of color. In the center of the table was a chipped glass vase of fresh wildflowers. On the dirt floor were colorful braided rag rugs. Someone had, with great care, created a home.

"I had no idea anyone lived on Shadow."

"No one does."

"Then why all this?" He gestured about the cozy room. "Someone has been here, and from the looks of the flowers, no later than yesterday."

"Are you sure?"

"Of course." He touched a flower with the tips of his fingers. "Good grief! These flowers have been preserved."

"Yes, they have, but naturally. They've been sitting on that table for nearly a hundred years."

"That's impossible."

"The tables and the chairs, even the cushions and the pillows are older than that. This is the cave of the MacLaren."

Adam was drawing his camera from its case and loading it with the proper film as she spoke. When he had made his adjustments and settings, he began to shoot rapidly and expertly, recording this room and its furnishings for his book. Once he touched a dirt wall, dusted off his fingers, then returned to his photographs. Finally satisfied that he had all he needed, he put his equipment away.

"Can you tell me about the MacLaren?"

Tracy nodded. "Come and sit."

"If the cushions are that old, won't we hurt them?"

"No." She waited while Adam laid aside his camera, then lowered himself cautiously into the chair beside her.

"If the MacLaren no longer lives here, does someone come to take care of it?"

"The only care any of us takes of it is to leave it alone."

"Who was MacLaren and why did he live up here on Shadow? Surely he would rather be in the valley among friends." As Tracy slowly shook her head, he leaned back into the surprising comfort of the old chair. Patiently he waited for her to begin her story.

"Nobody knew who he was, or when he came, or even where he came from. He was seldom in the valley, so no one knew how long he'd been here before they saw him. He shunned the company of others and rarely spoke. When he needed coffee or sugar, or any other staples, he came down off the mountain, wearing the tattered blue and green plaid of his clan. Children cried when they saw him, pregnant women hid their eyes, and even men turned away.

"He was a giant of a man and obviously very strong, but he was hideously scarred. The settlers in the valley speculated that he'd been burned and tortured, but no one ever really knew for certain. For years he lived here in squalor, with hardly the barest necessities, until he found his Laura.

"When he was checking his traps late one evening, he found her wandering in a heavy snow. She had no memory of who she was, except that her name was Laura. She couldn't remember where she had been or where she was going, but she must have been lost for a long time. Because of the constant glare of light on the snow, she was blind.

"MacLaren took her first to his cave, this cave. He treated her for frostbite, and then later for pneumonia. For two days he cared for her. When he realized he needed help, he took her into the valley to an herb woman. No one ever understood how he got her down the mountain alive, but he did. He stayed for days with the healer, doing exactly as she asked.

"Laura was conscious for short periods of time. She would cling to his hand and refuse to let him leave her side. When she lapsed into unconsciousness, she called constantly for Dougal. The people in the valley learned later that this was the MacLaren's Christian name."

Tracy shifted in her seat, looked slowly about the room, then continued with her narrative. "When Laura's fever finally broke, the MacLaren made his preparations to leave. She cried and pleaded with him to stay with her. At first he was adamant that he must go, then in the face of her tears, he relented.

"For three more days he stayed with her, baring his ugliness to those who came and went. He fed her, changed her bed, and brushed her long black hair. When he knew she was regaining her strength, he again made ready to return to Shadow. Laura didn't cry and plead for him to stay with her this time. Instead, she insisted that he let her come back to the mountain with him. He refused, and Laura told him she loved him.

"The legend says that he knelt by her bedside, stroking her hair with his big, mutilated hands. There were tears streaming down his face as he told her how ugly he was, and that when she could see she would hate him. Laura listened very patiently and didn't interrupt, but waited for him to finish.

"When he left her side and shouldered his pack, she watched him until he reached the door. Then she spoke for the first time since he had refused to take her with him."

"What did she say?" Adam prompted when Tracy paused.

'I've been able to see for the past three days, and you're the most beautiful man I've ever known.'"

"Surely he couldn't leave her then."

"No. He married her that very day, and when the snow melted and the trails were clear again, he brought her here. There were those who swore that over the next three years the MacLaren did change. Perhaps he wasn't as beautiful as Laura thought him, but he was less ugly.

"When the weather permitted he brought her down to the valley to shop, for dances, or simply to visit. Laura was a gay little thing, and even he began to fit in.

"Then in the dead of night, during a bitter cold winter, the MacLaren came down from Shadow without Laura. He carried a very small bundle in his arms. He stopped at Jenny Brown's house. When she answered his knock, he very gently placed the bundle in her arms. There were tears on his face and in his voice when he said, 'Keep her well until I return.' Then he turned and walked away.

"There was a tiny baby wrapped inside a delicate handmade quilt. She was dressed only in a nightshirt and a diaper. A locket was wrapped around her wrist. Jenny took her in and cared for her with all the love of a childless woman, and all the while she waited for his return. But no one ever saw him again."

"What do you think happened?"

"No one knows. Perhaps Laura was lost or taken and the MacLaren went after her. We do know that loving him as she did, she would never have left him willingly. We know, too, that he would search until he found her.

"Now Shadow keeps their home as they left it. Waiting for their return."

"But the flowers . . . it was winter."

"No one can explain that. Perhaps the MacLaren came back for a time in the spring, or perhaps . . ." Tracy shrugged and stopped.

Adam had listened spellbound; now he felt a need to move, to shake off the last sad note. As he walked about the room his gaze fell on the bright plaid and shiny wood of bagpipes. He didn't touch them. "His, of course."

"Yes. He played them for Laura."

"I see." Adam wandered restlessly again, then paused. "You never said what happened to the child."

"She was well cared for. Jenny Brown had lost all her children in an epidemic the year before. The baby was a godsend. She grew to womanhood, married, and had children without ever leaving the valley. She's still living, but she's quite old and completely blind."

"Opal."

"Yes."

Again, Adam prowled the room. Tracy watched but said nothing. Twice he touched the smooth dry walls of the cave, and once the floor. She heard him mutter, "It must be the dry air and the altitude that's preserved it so well."

Prudently Tracy offered no comment.

The trek back down the trail was easier and much quieter. Adam was withdrawn and introspective, as he had been since putting away his camera after taking a few last photographs of the cave, and Tracy was reluctant to break into his thoughts.

Lunch was a quick but hearty affair. Each ate with good appetite, then they stretched out side by side on a blanket Adam had spread by the stream. A pale sun bore down on them and the water sang as it rushed over its rocky bed. It wasn't long before Tracy drifted into a restful but light sleep.

The softest of caresses drew her from her dreams. When she opened her eyes Adam was leaning over her, his smile filling her world. "I always wanted to wake a sleeping beauty with a kiss. Or should I say lazy beauty?"

Tracy's mouth curved into a smile. "I think I've just been given a left-handed compliment."

"Of course. I'm left-handed, hadn't you noticed?"

"I've noticed."

"If you knew what I've been noticing, you'd consider getting up from your bed of leisure and getting on with the business of this trip. What have you planned?" he asked as he helped her up.

"There's one more thing I want to show you." Tracy folded the blanket and carried it back to the camp. "It isn't far, and the climb's not half so bad as the one to the crest. You needn't bother with refilling your canteen. There'll be plenty of fresh cold water."

"How long will it take to see it?"

"Not long."

"Another cave?"

"No."

"Another legend?"

"No."

"You aren't going to tell me, are you?"

"Nope."

"You do love a good mystery, don't you?"

"Don't you know that the way to a man's heart is through a good mystery?"

"Uh . . . I don't think you've got that quite right."

"Haven't I?" Tracy winked and set off across the meadow in the opposite direction from the one they had taken earlier. She skipped lightly over a stone, then began to whistle a happy, tuneless melody.

Adam stood as he was, gladness rising within him. Then he crossed the meadow after her.

Seven

"This is it?"

"Sure is." Tracy ducked her head to hide her grin.

"Do you mean you brought me all the way over the trail and through that infernal briar patch to show me another trail?" Adam loftily ignored her giggle at his use of one of Sarah's favorite words. "Even as trails go, this one is particularly nondescript."

"For heaven's sake, Adam!" Tracy scolded playfully. "Stop growling like a bear with a sore toe and take your pictures. You'll be glad you did."

"Do you promise?"

"I solemnly promise."

"I'll hold you to that. But I don't think anything will make me glad to have shots of that misbegotten place."

"Have I steered you wrong yet?"

"No."

"Then trust me."

"I do, darlin'. With my life." Adam grinned at her and began to photograph the path from varied angles.

Leaning against a large smooth boulder that dwarfed her, Tracy lifted her face to the light, absorbing the warm rays that filtered through the low-growing trees. Totally relaxed, with one foot firmly on the ground and the other resting against the stone, she listened to the familiar sounds of Adam at work.

With my life. His words were in the whispered sounds of the swaying pine and the rustle of the oak. The softest of smiles crept over her face.

Choosing his composition, judging the light and using shadows for contrast, Adam carefully photographed the terrain. The ugliness of the surroundings wouldn't matter; they would be interesting. He had only been gruffly teasing and he knew Tracy understood. In their time together on the mountain, an easy camaraderie had grown between them. More than anything he liked to see the slow, teasing smile light her eyes, followed by a low, husky chuckle. This was the Tracy of whom he hoped to see more, the one he feared he would lose when they left the mountain. Tomorrow was their last day, and a slow dread was beginning to build within him.

He swung his camera toward what had rapidly become his favorite subject. How many women, he wondered, could be so lovely or so desirable dressed in heavy jeans and a plaid hunter's shirt? Despite the boots that could not by any stretch of the imagination be called dainty, she seemed fragile. A smudge of dirt marked her cheek and a leaf was caught in the braid that lay against her breast.

His eyes were drawn to her slender waist, the narrow hips, then again upward to the full breasts that pushed against the soft fabric of her shirt. With each slow indrawn breath her shapeliness was evident. He was certain her breasts were bare, but the shirt was nothing if not concealing. The image of how she might look with it open, then discarded, was something of which dreams were made.

Two more shots, then he closed the shutter and quietly walked over to her. He lifted the braid and with its end he traced down her forehead to the tip of her nose. Tracy smiled but didn't open her eyes or move.

"You've been gathering leaves with your braid."

"Have I?"

"Just one, but it was quite fetching. Like an emerald clinging to black silk."

"Shadow brings out the poet in you," she said with a soft laugh.

"Not Shadow. You."

Tracy opened her eyes. Adam was leaning against the stone, looking down at her. "Am I fetching, Adam?"

"Very! Particularly with this smudge right here." With his thumb he brushed away the loose dirt. "There. Now you look almost presentable again. What would you do without me?"

"I don't know." The words were not a whisper, but they were said in such a low voice, Adam wasn't sure he understood.

He searched her face gravely, hoping against hope that he could believe what he saw. Shaken, his desire for her an almost tangible thing; he wanted desperately to draw her away from the stone, to hold her close, to make love to her. He wanted it as he had never wanted anything before, but he knew he mustn't. Instead he leaned forward, kissed her lightly on her upturned nose, then moved away.

"Do I get to see what's on this pitiful trail sometime today, or do you plan to become a lady of leisure, basking in the sun?"

Tracy instantly accepted his change of mood. Her expression was mischievous as she straightened away from her resting place. "I don't think that's the way any self-respecting leadee should speak to his leader. He might get left behind."

"Perish the thought. But, 'leadee'?"

"I didn't forget." She laughed at his frowning, questioning look. "I simply made it up."

Subconsciously Adam had tensed at her use of the word. Now he relaxed and his laughter joined hers. "You're a sharp little cookie, aren't you?"

"If you say so." Still laughing, she moved around him and up the trail.

Adam was unashamed of the sudden restriction in his throat. For the first time, Tracy had teased about her disability. Perhaps it was a sign that her paralyzing fear of its return was lessening. Perhaps she was one step closer to becoming the whole woman, a combination of the kind and generous tracker he had met in the valley and the enchanting, desirable Tracy he had discovered on Shadow. For her own happiness and his as well, he hoped he wasn't mistaken.

"Now who's standing about like a lazy layabout?" she called back to him. "If you want to see what's beyond here, now's the time."

"I believe my lady of leisure has become my fearless leader again," he answered lightly. "Never let it be said that this leadee didn't follow his leader into the rigors of yon dull, drab pathway."

"If that's some sort of quote, I think I missed something."

"Nothing to worry yourself about." Adam knew she didn't realize what she had said, that her teasing had been spontaneous. His step was buoyant as the spark of happy hope that had glowed faintly in his heart burst into full flame. With patience she would be his.

At the edge of the path, he stopped to stand just below where she waited. "You remind me of Summer when she has some surprise for me," he said. "There have been several times here on Shadow when I've seen flashes of the child you must have been. And each is more enchanting than the last."

"Just don't pat me on the head and call me a good girl." She wrinkled her nose, but her eyes held a light-hearted amusement.

"Never! But I would like to take you to bed and kiss you goodnight."

"Take?"

"Tuck."

"That's better."

"A slip of the tongue." Adam smothered a grin.

"Of course," Tracy replied airily, then turned and with a quick step raced to the top of the dusty track. From her lofty stand she looked down at him. "Now that you've managed to untangle your tongue, come on up. There's something I'd like to show you."

"Right behind you." As nimbly as she had, he scaled the rocky path and joined her on the ridge.

"Look." Tracy turned and extended her arm in a sweeping gesture.

Following the motion of her hand, Adam saw a part of Shadow unlike any he had seen before. At his feet lay a tiny valleylike hollow. Tall, lush grass undulated as the mountain breeze rippled over it. Except for the dusty track that wandered in and among the scattered trees, this place was as richly green as all else had been bleak and bare.

Adam reached for his camera as Tracy explained the hidden valley. "The Applachians are a mature chain of mountains and quite old. Most have rounded peaks and are densely covered by trees. Shadow was probably just like all the others until something happened—an earthquake, a massive landslide. Something nearly ripped her apart, defacing her, leaving her as we know her."

"Except this part."

"Yes. This small section was spared. From it you can see that Shadow was once a beautiful woman." Tracy turned toward him. "There's more. Would you like to go down now?"

"Okay." He slid his camera back into its case and took her hand. "Shall we?"

Like young lovers, they wandered hand in hand down the path and through this highland vale. The trees were tall and straight, the trunks of the hardwoods greater than a man's arm span.

"This is as far as we go," Tracy said as they rounded the last turn.

The trail ended abruptly at a sturdy wooden railing. When Adam stepped closer he was looking down into a deep gorge that was wild and untamed. A river of white water clawed and churned through the chasm, twisting and turning and taking with it everything that stood in its path. Even trees and boulders were swept away. With jagged cliffs and deeply carved walls, it was a primordial scene.

"This is how the world must have looked in the beginning," he murmured, automatically reaching for his camera.

"It's like time stood still," Tracy said, then, not wishing to distract him, she stepped away. She sat down on a flat stone that looked like a natural bench.

"Do many people come here?"

"Only an occasional hiker, or maybe a hunter. It's not exactly in the flow of traffic."

"Then why this guard rail?"

"Because even the valley has its share of foolish people who do foolish things."

Something in her tone disturbed him. He carefully set his camera aside and sat by her on the stone. Taking her hand in his and weaving his fingers through hers, he held her arm against his side.

Tracy looked down at his broad, strong hand and the lean fingers that had caressed her. "Maybe the altitude has gotten to us." Her laugh was wobbly and not quite believable.

"How so?"

"Already today you've compared me to a child. Then we spend the afternoon holding hands like a couple of teenagers."

"More of us should rediscover the child in ourselves, Tracy. And I like the feel of your hand in mine." Refusing to be diverted, he then asked softly, "What happened here?"

She would have drawn away from him, but he refused to release her. "The purpose of this trip was to show you something unique and beautiful, not to drag out old stories better forgotten."

"I'd like to know," Adam said gently, persuasively. He brushed his thumb over her wrist in a slow stroke that was as exciting as it was soothing.

The slight nod of her head was followed by a deep shuddering sigh as she yielded. "Years ago a careless young teenager wandered too near the brink of this ravine. Before she could catch hold or regain her balance, she slipped over the edge."

"You, Tracy?"

"Yes. I was seventeen and this was one of my favorite places. No one knew I came here and I could dream the dreams of a young girl."

"Were you hurt?"

"No. There's a ledge just below. Not so far down that the fall did more than bruise me, but too far for me to climb out. There were no plant or roots, and the soil was so hard, it might have been granite. My hands were the only tools I had. For what seemed like an eternity I tried to claw my way out."

A sound of distress rumbled in Adam's throat. He had no need for her to tell him of fear and desperation, or of torn nails and bleeding fingers. His hand tightened protectively around hers.

"There was no use in calling out. No one would have ever heard. It could've easily been days before I was found . . . or even never.

"When I was exhausted, when I thought there was nothing left for me to do, I found the knife. It was wedged between two stones at my feet. It was old and rusty, but the most wonderful thing I'd ever seen. Using it to make handholds, I literally carved my way up the face of the cliff."

She lifted her head, her eyes meeting his for the first time since she had begun her story. Memories of the terror were as vivid as if it had happened a day ago.

"Oh, God." Adam drew her to him, holding her close,

resting his head against hers. "Sometimes I wonder how you've survived this monster."

"Shadow's no monster," she said firmly. "What I needed she gave to me. She always has."

Accepting, for now, Adam said no more. His hands moved gently over her back, stroking her braid down to her waist.

Tracy's arms stole about him, her fingers caressing the hard swell of his muscles. Her head rested against his heart and her disquieting memories were tempered by its steady beat. The trauma and the fear of that experience still had the power to unnerve her. Except for the accident that had very nearly taken her life and mind, it had been her closest brush with death.

"I wonder if Shadow would give me what I need?" His voice was deeply resonant in her ear.

"And what might that be?"

"A kiss."

"Perhaps Shadow wouldn't, but I will. But what of our resolution?"

"Resolutions were made to be broken," he muttered as he tilted her chin so he could look down into her face. His eyes had grown smoky with desire and he leaned close to her. "Kiss me, Tracy," he murmured against her lips. "Kiss me as if you mean it."

Tracy needed no other invitation. Her arms closed tighter about him, her fingers crumpling the fabric of his shirt. Her lips parted eagerly, even as he was seeking the sweetness of her mouth. Resolutions were, indeed, made to be broken and cast to the wind, she decided, as she and Adam joined together in a wild enchantment.

Adam's hand slipped slowly from the scar down her body. At her breast he paused to brush lightly over its fullness, then with shaking fingers he unbuttoned her shirt. His hands slipped inside and closed over her warm flesh. With a soft sigh Tracy moved instinctively to give him free access to her body.

A joy like none she had ever known surged through

her at his first intimate touch. His hands were a sweet caress to the ache growing inside her. Sweeter still were the softer touch of his lips and the rasp of his tongue as he kissed a proud nipple. Her fingers laced through his hair to cradle him to her, to offer him herself.

He moved away from her with deliberate slowness, his eyes seeking hers. Never looking away, he traced the contours of her face with his fingers, lingering at her trembling mouth. He drew her close and kissed her gently—once, twice—then moved away again. His thumbs met at the base of her throat where her pulse beat raggedly, then he slid his hands down her bare skin. As they closed reverently over her breasts, he stared at her intently, needing to know that her desire matched his. He was rewarded by a sudden flaring in her dark eyes and a soft sigh. A shiver of delight rippled through her body and her breathing quickened. Then, as he caressed the sensitive breasts, she drew in a sharp breath.

"Tracy?" He drew back quickly, his eyes seeking what his fingers had found. Small red marks marred her dusky skin. "My beard! I hurt you! Why didn't you tell me?"

Tracy looked down at herself in surprise, feeling no shame that he was looking hungrily at her even in his concern. "I—I didn't know."

"Damn beard! I'll shave it first thing when we get back to camp."

"No!" She rubbed the coarse stubble with the palm of her hand. "It'll soften as it grows. You didn't hurt me, Adam. Really, you didn't."

"Perhaps not." He drew the edges of her shirt together and began to button it. "But I would if we continued as we were."

"Adam?" She looked at him with such pleading that his resolve was almost destroyed.

"No, love, not yet. This is a special place for you; you're feeling the backlash of your memories. I offered comfort and, perhaps, security, and you're grateful. I don't want gratitude from you, Tracy. It wouldn't be enough."

She remembered her own words from the night of the dance—that it was too soon, that their emotions were in turmoil—and realized that he was right. She was almost sure she could cope with having the little that could be hers before Adam left Shadow. But almost wasn't good enough. She must be certain, or this could destroy her.

"If you're ready," he said, lifting her face to his, "now that I have my sanity restored, what's next for the day?"

"Nothing on the legends," Tracy whispered, still in the grip of her own emotions. "But there's a place I'd like to check before we go down to camp."

"All right," he agreed.

"I should warn you, it'll be a long hike and there's nothing you could use in your book." She paused. "Maybe I should leave it for another time. I could, you know."

"Shh, Tracy love. Just who is it that you're trying to discourage? Yourself or me?"

"A little of both, I guess," she admitted ruefully.

"You obviously do want to see this place, or you wouldn't have brought it up, and I don't mind, so what's the problem?"

"Not anything, I suppose." She stood up, feeling lost without his touch. "We should leave now if we expect to make camp by nightfall."

The only visible signs that the old derelict had once been a home were part of a roofline and an old stone chimney that was still standing. Tons of rock and dirt had been torn away from the mountain and buried it. A flower bed in what had once been the yard had been weeded. Though no one lived there, someone still came and cared for the area.

"I had no idea that anyone had lived on Shadow so recently," Adam said. "Did you know them?"

"I lived here," Tracy answered. "With Grandfather."

Her tone was perfectly level and completely emotionless, but Adam could feel her loss. "When?"

"Three years ago." She stared at the ruin that had been her home for many years. "He's still there. I like to think he's sitting in his favorite chair where he sat every evening." With a faraway look in her eyes she gazed up at the mountain. "He would've been resting there when the mountain came down on him."

"Then Shadow took your grandfather?"

"No. She *kept* him." Tracy turned away. With her back to the cabin she relaxed. "He was very ill, Adam. He had been for quite some time. For the last year he was in almost unbearable pain. At first the drugs helped some, but he'd reached the stage where they no longer did anything. He never complained, but each day was a great agony. So Shadow gathered him to her and ended his suffering."

"You still miss him." Adam didn't need to ask. He simply read her face.

"Yes." She summoned her strength and faced the cabin again. "I'll always miss him. He taught me all I knew as a child. Then he became my courage and my salvation after the accident. But I could let him go, Adam. He'd lived a full, happy life. By sheer willpower he had stayed with me longer than we expected he could."

"Where were you when it happened?"

"He'd sent me across the valley to the workshop. He wanted me to do a carving that day. I think he knew what was coming, and he was ready. He felt I'd recovered enough that he could leave me."

"The workshop wasn't here?"

"It had been for a long time. Then he had an inexplicable desire to move it away from Shadow. He gave me no reason. He simply wanted it moved. I'm sure he knew the slide was coming and was saving his carving tools for me.

"The cabin and buildings at the other side of the valley

had been his. He lived there until my grandmother died; then he came to Shadow."

"Have you ever thought about returning yourself?"

"No. When Wolfe and I left here, I knew that I would never live on Shadow again."

"Where is Wolfe now?"

"He's here with my grandfather." Tracy turned toward a pile of small stones. "I brought him back to the person and the place he loved best. Wolfe loved me and took care of me, but he was truly the dog of the Forest Walker. They were two of a kind. Grandfather left him here only to watch after me a bit longer. Wolfe saw me through my grief and helped me accept Grandfather's death. He had been tired for a long time."

Adam took her cool, dry hand in his. "You've been fortunate in many ways."

"I know." Her fingers clung to his, but she said no more.

He waited patiently, watching her carefully. He could almost read her thoughts as she looked once more at the cabin, then at the grave of the dog, then at the flowers. He knew she had planted them. He could see her love in each blossom.

"Are you ready to return to camp?"

"Yes." She clasped his hand more firmly in her own. "I'm ready."

The sun had begun to sink beyond the mountain when they arrived back at the meadow. The stones in the stream bed glistened with the fresh moisture of the cool day. Tracy again instructed Adam to follow her path, stepping exactly where she did as they crossed.

With the ease of experience she crossed without mishap. Adam was not so fortunate. When the opposite shore was nearly within his reach, his foot slipped. Amid an inelegant waving of arms and a frantic search for firm footing, he fell with more splash and less dignity than before.

"Adam! Not again!" Tracy put her hands on her hips. "This is becoming a habit. Too busy protecting your cameras to catch yourself?"

"So it would seem," he replied dryly.

"Are you hurt this time?"

"Only my pride."

"Then aren't you going to get up?"

"Not for a minute." His gaze moved over her slowly. Instinctively, though she knew she had been well beyond the reach of the scattering water, she looked down at her shirt.

A flush spread over her cheeks as she realized that Adam had read her thoughts. To hide her embarrassment she said quickly, "Are you going to sit there all evening?"

"No."

"Then what on earth are you doing?"

"I'm thinking."

"You *like* to sit in cold water to think?"

"Shh. I'm creating a legend."

"A legend!"

"Um-hm. One that says when a flatlander photographer falls into the creek for the second time in two days, he must sit there until he's kissed by a pretty, dark-haired woman."

"Adam, don't be ridiculous. Get up before you freeze."

"Can't."

"Come on. This isn't a joking matter. You might catch cold."

"I'm not joking. The legend says I can't get up until you kiss me."

Tracy's suppressed laughter broke free. "I think Shadow's finally gotten to you."

Adam only smiled, crossed his arms over his chest, and waited. Water swirled and eddied about him, but he paid no attention to it.

Accepting defeat, Tracy walked back across the stones. When she reached him she sat on the one closest to him. Without a trace of a smile she cupped his cheek in her palm and touched his lips softly with her own. Drawing back, she brushed a strand of hair from his forehead and regarded him intently. She whispered his name as she leaned forward to kiss him again.

Her mouth was warm and seeking against his. Her tongue caressed him fleetingly, like rough velvet, then she moved away. Her eyes never left his as she rose and held out her hand.

Adam was as bemused as she as he accepted her help. Together they crossed the stream to the campsite.

For the first time since they had come to Shadow, Adam could see that Tracy was tired. Though she didn't limp, she did move her right leg carefully. At supper her hand had trembled so badly, she had put down her cup and hadn't take it up again. She disappeared for a quick bath and shampoo in the stream, and by the time she reappeared, wearing her sweatsuit, and with a towel wrapped around her hair, she moved with a marked slowness that worried Adam. Strain showed in her face and dark smudges had appeared under her eyes.

While she'd been gone Adam had built the fire to a strong, warm blaze, for there was the promise of fall in the night. He was concerned that the toll of the day, both emotional and physical, might make her easy prey for a chill.

"Hi," he said as she approached the fire. "Feeling better?"

"Much. It always helps to wash away the trail dust."

"Come sit by the fire." He patted the sleeping bags he had spread out side by side while she'd been gone.

If Tracy considered it strange that they would not be sleeping as they had the night before, she made no comment and sat down beside him.

"Are you warm enough?" he asked in a voice low with worry.

"The fire's nice. I'm very comfortable, Adam."

"Then rest, love. I'll be back before you know it." He gathered up his own soap and towel and quickly disappeared in the direction Tracy had come from.

Long after he had gone she sat staring into the fire, fascinated by the dancing flames. Her thoughts were on the day and Adam. She remembered how he had looked kneeling by the stream in the early morning light, how he had likened her to Alice, and his gift of a flower. Even now it rested, safe and protected, in her first aid kit.

She remembered, also, his worry for her at the MacLaren's cave and his lovemaking at the ravine. *With my life.* The phrase leaped into her mind, softening a bit of the tired strain in her face.

"Tracy?" Adam stood across the fire from her. His chest was bare, the curling black hair showing none of the silver she had expected. His fresh dry jeans were beltless and rode low over his lean hips. His dark skin seemed darker still because of the pristine white towel hanging about his neck. His eyes still held the same caring concern she had seen at the cabin and by Wolfe's grave.

"I'm all right, Adam," she assured him. "I'm only tired."

With a start she realized she'd made no move to take the towel from her hair, nor to comb out the tangles. How long, she wondered, had she been staring into the fire thinking of Adam?

"You're sure?" he asked.

"Absolutely." To prove her point, she unwrapped the towel and shook her hair free, then began combing it.

"Wait." Adam quickly shrugged into a lightweight sweatshirt. "Let me."

He settled himself behind her, drawing her back between his bent legs. He took the comb from her and carefully worked through each tangle. Once he left her to stack more wood on the fire, then returned to his self-appointed task. Long after the snarls had been controlled, he continued to comb the flowing strands in long sweeping strokes.

Tracy grew visibly less tense and more rested. When her hair was dry, Adam put away the comb. With his fingertips he began to massage her temples, then down her jaw to the base of her neck and across her shoulders.

"Mmm, nice."

"Always at your service, my lady." The pressure of his touch remained unchanged as he worked the corded muscles of her neck. Only her soft sighs of pleasure and the crackle of the fire could be heard.

Tracy was never really aware of when it changed. She never knew when the contentment became a wild longing. Suddenly she desperately wanted him to answer the surging cry of her body. More than anything in her life, she needed Adam.

But could she love him and let him go? Could she return to her cloistered life unscathed if she listened to her heart? Could there be life for her after Adam?

"Better?" His voice broke into her thoughts and when she looked at him, she knew her decision must come soon.

"Yes. Much better. Thank you."

"You seemed so far away. What were you thinking?"

"I . . . Not really anything." She hated to dissemble, but would he understand the direction of her thoughts? Did she understand?

She leaned forward and picked up a large chip of wood. Without thinking, she reached to her belt for her knife. Old habits died hard. In the past when she had been troubled, she'd turned to the soothing and restful carving. If the strength in her hand seemed in danger of faltering, as it did tonight, she denied its weakness by plying her knife. In concise strokes, she created from the chunky block of wood a crude but delicate flower. It would take hours for it to become the finished product, but for now it was simply her therapy.

"Alice's flower?" Adam asked.

"It will be, but not for a while yet."

"It looks good already to me."

"The shape is barely there," she said with a slight smile.

"This is the knife you found on the ledge."

"I've kept it with me since that day." she continued working the wood with the knife, but twice she nearly dropped it.

"Let it go for the night, darling." His hand closed over hers, stopping it. "It's late. Why don't we turn in? We're making an early start in the morning, aren't we?"

Tracy sheathed her knife and put away the flower. "You're right. Tomorrow will be a long day."

He kissed her lightly on her cheek, then stood and smoothed his sleeping bag.

"Adam." She waited until he looked at her. "I am tired, but it's been a nice day."

"A beautiful day," he agreed, but knew that she had been the beauty of it.

Eight

The fire had died to dusty gray embers and still Adam was awake. The night was clear and through the trees he could see stars that seemed near enough to touch. The sounds of the forest had grown strangely muted in the thickening dark. Only Tracy, who lay close by him, was reality.

"Adam?" His name, as she said it, was a beautiful sound.

"I thought you were asleep."

"Only resting. You haven't slept?"

"No. I was watching the night."

There was no answer, only the slow, even rise and fall of her breathing. He wondered if she had at last fallen asleep.

"I've been meaning to thank you." Her voice filled the darkness.

"Thank me?" He turned his head to look blankly at her. "For what, Tracy?"

"For not judging me as others have. You knew of the accident and the rumors, yet you never condemned me."

"I wish that were completely true. I'm afraid I have my feet of clay too. I had my doubts. Don't you remember? I acted like a thirty-six-year-old child."

"You mean about Jed." The day at the post office and Adam's strange reaction rushed through her mind.

"I thought you might be his mistress."

"What changed your mind?"

"You did. You told me quite bluntly that you belonged to no one, and that there was nothing but friendship between you."

"Just like that? You believed me?"

"Yes."

Tracy was quiet for a long while, savoring the gift of his trust, yet wondering how he had dealt with her past. "Have you been curious about what happened years ago?"

"At first I was," he admitted truthfully, "but when I learned your grandfather's identity, I understood."

"So you know about my parents?"

"Anyone who's ever been involved in the movie industry knows their story. The young actress, daughter of a prominent filmmaker, who was becoming a person of note in her own right. Her love for a man of Indian descent, the son of a famous artist, one who had little use for the trappings of her public life. They married, and though she still made an occasional film, she was never a part of the Hollywood scene. Then ten or twelve years ago they perished together in a private plane crash." Adam shifted restlessly. "We all knew their story, or thought we did. Nobody ever knew there was a child."

"I was a well-kept secret. Mother had grown up being so constantly in the public eye that she wanted to protect me from it. We lived here in the valley, where I spent a happy, uneventful childhood, free of the circus atmosphere so many show-business children face."

"Yet you became an actress yourself."

"I was young and impressionable, Adam. I had this glorious idea that I would continue in my mother's footsteps, but without the benefit and help of her name. I chose to use my middle name for anonymity."

"Why wasn't your identity revealed later? It could've

answered so many of the rumors. The public would've understood that your relationship with the producer was innocent, that he was your mother's brother."

"At first those who knew were more concerned with whether I would live than with the gossip. When I started to recover it was too late to bother. The furor had died down and no one wanted to stir it up again for any reason. We simply lived from day to day, and when he could, Grandfather brought me back here to Shadow.

"The valley people knew about me, and they understood. It was all that mattered—until you came." Tracy's voice trembled and broke on the last words.

"Come here." Adam lifted her, bag and all, to bring her closer to him. She made no protest, but quietly accepted the warmth of his embrace.

"Comfortable?" he asked.

"Mmm." Tracy moved closer into the curve of his shoulder. "But are you?"

"How could I not be when I have you in my arms?" He smoothed a strand of hair from her face with his lips. "You say the people of the valley understood about you. Did they understand the aphasia?"

"Not at first. Grandfather explained to them what it was, how it would affect me, and what my recovery would be like. They learned even more by being with me and listening to me. I'm sure I tried their patience, but no one was ever unkind to me."

"Still, it must've been terrible."

"It was. I won't deny that. It was painfully frustrating, and above all, frightening. I was a prisoner of my own mind. I knew what I meant, what I wanted to say, but the words wouldn't come. Even with the speech therapy and the physical therapy, my progress seemed slow. I would've given up without Grandfather and Wolfe.

"Each day, with their help, the words became less elusive. With the carving my hand grew stronger. On my walks with Wolfe my step became surer. Gradually the agnosia faded. I relearned the landmarks and he had to lead me home less and less often, until finally he became my companion rather than my guide.

"I'll never be as strong on the right side as I was, and I'll always have to speak slower, but I'm considered to be recovered. I've stabilized at this level, and I'm fortunate. Some aphasics never recover at all."

By habit, Adam's hand had found the scar. His fingers brushed over it absently, then down the white streak of hair that met it. "Do you think that the concentration the carving required might've stimulated your thought processes?"

"That's my reasoning, though the doctors have never ventured any sort of opinion. Their only comment is that due to some circumstances I've achieved an amazing recovery, far better than they ever hoped for."

"Over the years you must've accumulated quite a number of carvings."

"I have a veritable workshop full of them," Tracy said with a pleasant laugh. "They range from worse than the flower you saw a while ago to those displayed at the dance."

"I'd like to see them."

"They're at the cabin, but you can see them whenever you like."

"Few people outside the valley ever see them, do they, Tracy?"

"No."

"Why not?" he asked gently. "Why won't you share your talent? To have something as beautiful as one of your carvings would bring one a great deal of pleasure."

"I've shown and sold a few pieces in the past. Grandfather's needs were simple, so he kept very little of what he earned over the years. When he became so ill and the bills mounted, I sent a sampling of my carvings to the gallery where you saw 'A Vixen at Play.' They earned enough to keep him as comfortable as possible for as long as he lived. That was enough."

"Talent such as yours shouldn't be kept hidden," he

said, his tone almost clipped. "If you won't sell any of them, why won't you at least show them?"

"I can't." Tracy pulled away from him and sat up, staring into the dying coals. "I have no desire to spend long hours confined in a gallery."

"You wouldn't have to be there." Adam leaned forward to sit shoulder to shoulder with her. "The artist needn't be present when the work is shown."

"No! I couldn't do that! Each piece represents the regaining of some part of myself. They aren't just blocks of wood that've been whittled into some cute, little shape." Tracy's bitter tone matched her expression. "I couldn't just send them for strangers to stare at and not understand what they mean. I couldn't stand for them to be gaped at. It would be too much like baring my soul to the world."

"Tracy, Tracy." He rested a comforting hand on her shoulder. "No one could look at your work and feel as cold as that. Show the carvings. Come and watch the faces of those who see them. I think you'll be surprised at the emotions you inspire."

"No!" She shrugged his hand away. "That's impossible. I'm not leaving here for any art show."

Adam was startled by her vehemence. She was wrong and he knew it. She had no concept of the power of her own work. In time he would show her, he promised himself. He would share with her the pleasure of knowing her artistry was appreciated and treasured. Someday he would, but not yet. As with his love, this, too, would take time.

"Come, love." He firmly drew her stiff, resisting body back into his arms. "We won't speak of it anymore!"

Slowly, with a soft sigh she relaxed against him. Neither knew how long he held her. The last glowing coal had long since died and the sky had begun to brighten with the hint of false dawn before Adam spoke.

"Tomorrow we go the other side of Shadow."

"Yes. Many of her legends are tinged with sadness. Tomorrow I'll show you a happy one."

"Will the trail be difficult?"

"Yes."

"Then we both should get some rest."

"I know."

Neither moved. Adam was reluctant to relinquish her even for the needed sleep. Tracy had found a comfort in his arms that nothing could match.

"Could you sleep now?"

"Perhaps."

"If I hold you, could you?"

"Yes."

Adam pulled the rumpled sleeping bag around them and leaned farther back against his makeshift pillow of clothes. Tracy's long body curled into his longer one. Her head was pillowed by his chest. Before sleep overtook him, Adam sensed when she slipped into drowsy oblivion. He smiled to himself in the darkness, thinking how well she suited him in every way.

Five lonely and anguished days later Adam climbed Shadow again, alone. The path was as he remembered, climbing slowly upward in a crazy, distorted angle. It meandered around bends and by precipices for two miles, always obliquely rising. In direct contrast to the other side of Shadow, with its rocky slopes, this way was steeper and dotted by cliffs. Small chasms lined by shattered rock broke the trail repeatedly, forcing travelers to use an indirect route.

He was heading for the waterfall that Tracy had shown him that last day, drawn to it irresistibly. It was like a long, gleaming ribbon and could easily be seen from a great distance. It leaped from a high cliff and fell several hundred feet, then rushed again down the mountain. An outcropping of massive stone on the face of the cliff split it apart, channeling a small stream away and down a separate slope. Leaping from stone to stone in gentle cascades, it fell to a basin in a small plateau of its own.

The clear lake it formed was framed by stone worn smooth with age. The fronds of giant ferns dipped their leaves in rippling water that reflected rhododendron, tall and stately in their antiquity.

Tracy had laughed with childish delight at his speechless wonder when he had first glimpsed the lake. Again he had been reminded of the difference between this lively mountain woman and the remote valley woman. When they had left Shadow later that day, he had waited in dread for the reappearance of the aloof, withdrawn Tracy. He had watched for the calculated moves and the precise words, but they never came. She had, instead, remained the lighthearted woman who recognized her disabilities, but was not afraid. Even as they had bumped across the valley floor in her jeep, she had been the woman he'd discovered on Shadow. Adam had been exultant in his certainty that he had won.

After depositing him and his equipment at his cabin door, Tracy had blown him a kiss, waved jauntily, and left him.

In the days that followed, he had waited impatiently, listening for her familiar step on his porch. He had tried not to give in to the feeling that he had lost her, and today, frustrated and angry and restless from inactivity, he had come back to Shadow. With cameras and supplies he struggled toward the lake, intending to appease the caldron of seething emotions with work. Today he would continue alone the study that with Tracy had been exciting. More than once, when limbs slapped and briars clawed, he cursed himself, his cameras, and his own fertile mind for undertaking this project. Who was he to wrest from the mountain its secrets? How could he expect it to yield to him?

Another branch snapped back to graze his cheek above the beard. A sharp expletive broke from him, and again he wondered what he was doing there. He was a flatlander photographer who should stick to level ground. His legs ached, and he was hot and tired and irritable, his mood even blacker than when he had begun. Gradually the sharp incline began to lessen. Adam dodged under one last low-hanging branch and stepped into the clearing. He lowered his equipment to the ground, noting how the clear water sparkled in the bright sun and the echoing roar of the larger fall enveloped the plateau in a cocoon of muted sound.

As he swept this secret paradise with his sharp gaze, Adam realized that it was here that he had first seen the mountain through Tracy's eyes.

Beneath her harsh exterior, Shadow offered too many places of secret beauty to be ugly. But could he reconcile himself to the legends? He thought of the cave of the MacLaren, waiting safe and undisturbed; a rock-covered cabin where an old man's suffering had ended; an old and rusty knife that had saved Tracy's life. A soft smile replaced his scowl as he bent to pick a tiny flower. When he straightened he could almost believe he heard Alice laugh.

A splash of scarlet caught his attention. Barely visible at the foot of a huge boulder was a blanket. Stacked neatly on it were a sketch pad and charcoal. Eagerly he searched the shore and pathway for Tracy. Thinking that she might have scaled the rocky face of the wall to the top of Indian Maid Fall, he scanned the rock that jutted and tilted to form a natural stairway. The summit was deserted and only the sound of the falls broke the silence. His gaze was drawn downward, following the path of the water. It was then he saw her.

From beneath the fall she emerged, stepping lightly from one slippery stone to another. She stood poised before it, more a fairy creature than real. The rising mists of the water met the midday sun, wrapping her in a rainbow. Her long black hair fell wet over her shoulder and one bare breast. With a slow, leisurely brush of her hand, she flicked it back and in a fluid, arching dive cut cleanly through the lake water.

Adam walked to the water's edge. He watched spell-bound as she weaved her way in and out of the sunken rocks. Appearing, vanishing, reappearing, she had become a dusky-skinned mermaid, seductive yet strangely innocent.

A gentle splash and a quiet laugh sounded as she surfaced. Her arms flashed brown and strong as she swam to a large stone that hovered at the moss-covered banks. She shook back her hair as she rose from the water, then stepped onto the flat granite.

For a lingering moment she smiled down at her own image, then bent to shatter the reflection with the tip of her finger. Her husky laugh drifted through the air as she caught up a length of printed silk and knotted it low over her hips.

"Tracy," Adam said, stepping away from the concealing leaves of a huge fern.

She turned to him, making no move to cover herself. His eyes devoured her, sweeping over a face made more beautiful by its imperfections. Her breasts, with darkened crests taut from the chill of drying water, were firm yet full. A slender rib cage seemed far too frail to bear their weight. From a small waist, her body flared slowly, and the bare hip and thigh he glimpsed beneath the silk enticed him with their elegance.

"Adam."

His name on her lips broke the spell. Though he relaxed, he was no less bewitched by the sight of her. He knew there was sunlight in her hair, that a bird called. He heard the leaves rustle in the light breeze. The grass whispered and a cricket chirped, but it was not of his world. There was only Tracy as she moved to him. She stopped only a step away, waiting, soft-eyed and wistful.

The time was now, the moment that from the first day they had both known was inevitable. Adam gave a low, hoarse cry as he buried his hand in her hair, bunching it in his fist, reveling in the feel of it as he drew her to him. He filled his arms with her sleek loveliness, whispering soft words of promise and love.

Tracy's low murmuring answer was lost to him as she burrowed her face into his shirt. Her arms clung to him drawing him nearer, crushing her breasts against his chest.

"Your hair smells like wildflowers," he said.

"I was washing it."

"Under the falls?"

"Yes."

"I've missed you, Tracy."

"I know."

"Where did you go?"

"Back on the mountain, to think."

"About what?"

"This."

"And did you decide?" His heart seemed to stop as he waited an agonized eternity for her answer.

"I was coming to you."

"Now?"

"Yes." She drew away, her head tilted back, her eyes were held by his.

It was there at last. She had become the complete woman.

Tenderly, as if she would break, he touched her. Loving fingers stroked the jagged scar that was so much a part of her, then trailed down her cheek to her neck. The heel of his hand rested for a fleeting second at the first gentle swell of her breast, then he cupped the breast in his palm, molding the nipple in its hollow.

"Before you continue," she said, "I think I should tell you I've never made love before." Her tone, despite its halting breathlessness, was almost conversational.

The words hit him with the impact of an earthquake. Tremors of astonishment shook the hand at her breast. His fingers ceased their adoring stroke. His eyes were filled with wonder.

"Then the liberated woman was only the cloak worn by the shy young maiden." His hand moved lightly over her heart. Its cadence was strong and vigorous, and quickened beneath his touch.

"Not shy," she said gently. "Liberated. Most liberated. And confident enough in myself to feel no need to prove it." Her dark eyes glistened with warmth and love. "I have no fears of my body's needs," she half whispered.

"Then why?" Adam stared at her intently. She was beautiful. She was woman. She was bewilderment.

"There has never been anyone in my life before whose touch I wanted and needed. Desire alone was never enough, Adam."

She stood motionless before him, her tall, slender body proud and bare but for the scarflike silk that swayed alluringly about her. With a shuddering groan he reached for her, eager for the gift she offered.

His fingers sought again the soft perfection of her breasts, then traced the curve of her waist to the gentle swell of her hips. As he swept her up into his arms to carry her to the blanket, the colorful silk blew away in the breeze.

As she lay darkly inviting against the scarlet, Adam shrugged from his clothing. With skin as tawny as hers, he was her counterpart in silver. When he was naked, he stood transfixed by the treasure that was his for the taking. Much as he loved her and wanted her, he couldn't take that final step until he had one last sign that this was truly what she wanted.

"Adam." As though she understood his hesitancy, Tracy opened her arms to him.

With a ragged groan he sank down beside her. As his body touched hers, a sigh trembled through her. There was no need for more. With kisses and caresses he taught her the first of love. Slowly and with infinite care he awakened the passion that had been sleeping within her. Then with a soft sigh of his own he drew her beneath him.

"Oh, God." The low groan tore from his lips in agony. He tensed and would have pulled away, but Tracy's arms held him fast. "I can't, darling. I mustn't. You have no protec—"

"Shh." Her fingers at his lips stopped him. "It will be all right. I don't care."

"No! You could conceive."

"I don't care. Love me, Adam. Love me."

When he still would have resisted, she seduced him with an expertise that was astonishing. Having no understanding of the instincts that guided her, she lovingly tempted him beyond refusal.

"My love," he whispered as he answered her desire.

"Adam, I love you." Her words were lost in the mist and the rumble of the falls, but he heard and answered with body, heart, and soul.

Warmed by sunlight, Tracy turned, murmured a soft sound, then sought again the hard but comfortable slope of his broad chest. The chuckle that rumbled like a low growl against her ears was all part of a wonderful dream. A sleepy smile lifted her lips as she curled quite naturally against the long, lean body at her side. Her mouth brushed lightly over the bare skin.

There was no other sound as with loving hands Adam caressed her. He leaned over her, his free hand tangling in the long, shining black hair that spilled gloriously over the blanket. One kiss was given to each eyelid, one was brushed lightly over her cheek, then he whispered her name against her lips and took her once again to their own world of enchantment.

"Do you think she knows we're here?" Adam asked. He had awakened only minutes ago, and had spent the time watching Tracy sleeping with her head pillowed on his shoulder. When the ebony lashes had lifted to reveal her softly glowing dark eyes, he had kissed her flushed cheeks and asked his question.

"Do you mean Shadow?"

"No. The Indian maiden who came to the falls to bathe and found her true love. Do you think she knows we found each other here too?"

"I'd like to think that she does and that she's happy for us." Tracy leaned on her elbow and traced patterns in the pelt of dark hair that grew thickly on his chest. "It's the same color."

"Mmm?" Adam's silver eyes had turned to darkened steel as he quickened with desire.

"Your beard and your chest. Neither are red." Tracy sounded disappointed as she concentrated on the swirling thatch that narrowed to a line that reached beyond his waist.

"Tracy." Adam captured her wrist in his grasp. "I don't think you quite understand your own power yet. Perhaps we should have a swim, then go home."

He chuckled when her face clouded and her smile faded. He pulled her down to him, wrapping his arms about her. "You need time, love. Time for your body to heal."

"But you . . ." She blushed, dropped her eyes from his and mumbled, "Well, it only hurt for a moment."

His happy laughter rang out through the forest, startling a rabbit that was feeding at the edge of the glade. Adam rolled her onto the blanket, pinning her beneath him. His hands held each wrist above her head and he smiled down at her. "I love you, Tracy Walker. I love your heart and your body, but most of all your fighting spirit. To be brief, I love everything about you."

"I love you, Adam." Her look nearly made a mockery of his strength.

"Damn! If we don't go for a swim, it's very likely that I'll find myself doing exactly what I just said I shouldn't. Too bad the water's heated. I feel a definite need for a cold shower."

"There's always the waterfall," Tracy suggested, then laughed at his horrified look. She pushed him away in an unexpected move and bounded to her feet. "Last one in the lake is a lazy lover."

"Ah-ha!" Adam surged up to give chase. With the advantage of his longer legs he could overtake but not surpass her. Simultaneously they cut through the water in perfect dives.

Adam surfaced instantly. Turning all around, he searched the clear water for Tracy. Before he could find her she rose in front of him with a great splattering of water.

"So." He took her into his arms, pressing her hips close to his own. "Now that you have me in the lake, you plan to drown me."

"Never!" Tracy brushed the water from his face, then kissed him. "I have plans for you, but they have nothing to do with drowning." Her hands strayed over his ribs and down the curve of his hip.

He released her abruptly. "I think I *will* make use of the waterfall."

"I'll come with you."

"No!" He pointed an accusing finger at her. "You, you little witch, should get dressed immediately if you know what's good for both of us." He swam away toward the fall, muttering under his breath with every stroke he made.

Tracy watched him with her heart full of pride. He was a beautiful man, inside and out. And he could be hers for a time. Her smile was suddenly tinged with sadness as she turned toward the bank.

Two days of enchantment followed. The waterfall became their haven, and each time they loved, it was with a new intensity. On the third day they joined Jed and Liza on a picnic that had been planned long ago as a special treat for Summer.

"That's nice, Summer," Tracy said to the little girl. Tracy was sitting by the creek bank watching Summer sail the boats she had made out of hickory nut half shells, with leaves as their sails. "Your daughter's quite good at improvising, Adam."

"Of course. She gets it from her father."

"Is she as modest too?"

With his head resting in Tracy's lap, Adam was far too comfortable to rise to the bait of her teasing. He simply agreed. "Yes, that too."

Tracy laughed. "You're an idiot. But I love you."

Adam's eyes opened then. "I know. But it's like hearing it for the first time each time you say it." His voice grew husky. "Say it again."

"I love you." She whispered the words so none but he could hear.

"Tracy!" Summer stood before them, her hands on her hips in a childish imitation of Liza. "I've called you and called you. You're not paying any 'tention to me."

"I'm sorry, sweetheart. What did you want?"

"I wanted to know if we could go fishing now." Again, as the child spoke patiently, Tracy could almost hear her red-haired aunt saying the same words.

"I think we can. That is, if your father can do without a pillow for a while."

"It'll be difficult, but I suppose I can rough it if I must." He rolled away from Tracy and onto his feet in one smooth motion. He ruffled a curl that fell over Summer's eye. "Are you going to catch our supper for us, muffin?"

"Could I?" Her gray eyes that were so much like her father's sparkled with excitement. She turned to Tracy. "Could I really catch a fish for supper?"

"You might. There are some pretty big trout and catfish in the creek. Why don't we get started? Maybe we'll have a nice string of fish in time for supper. You catch them, your daddy can clean them, and I'll cook them. Deal?"

"Deal." Summer laughed and scampered to the tree where the fishing rods rested. "Which one can I use?"

"Why don't you take the shorter one. It fits you better."

"Tracy," Adam said softly. "I have news for you. I don't think I have the proper tools for cleaning a fish."

"Not to worry." Tracy looked toward her cabin that was barely visible through the heavy foliage of the oaks. "I have all you need."

"You're a woman of many talents, Tracy darlin'. A matchless tracker, an artist, a good cook, a true friend, a wonderful lover . . ."

"Adam! Hush, they'll hear you." Tracy glanced toward the couple who had just come from a trail that led through the woods. "Hello, Liza, Jed. Did you have a good walk?"

"It was wonderful," Liza said. "Jed showed me several plants that I might use for dye when I do my next weaving. It would be interesting to try to duplicate some of the old colors." Liza stopped short at Adam and Tracy's laughter. "*Now* what did I say?"

"Nothing, Liza," Adam said. "You just always shock me when you sound so much like you belong here."

"Maybe she does," Jed said, smiling brilliantly at Liza.

"We'll see," she said, a faint blush suffusing her face.

Looking from one to the other, Tracy realized that she had missed something. She had been so wrapped up in Adam for the past few days, she hadn't recognized the signs that were so obvious. Jed was in love with Liza, and if Tracy's eyes weren't deceiving her, his love was returned.

Tracy found herself wishing fervently that Jed and Liza would marry. Then Adam would come back to the mountain at least for visits. The thought lightened the small dark ray of sadness that edged every part of her days with him. Her gaze met his, and she found that he was watching her with a puzzled expression.

"I've got one! I've got one!" Summer's excited call

broke into the silence that had fallen between all of them. "Help! I can't hold him."

Adam and Jed ran to the child's side. Adam placed his hands on Summer's and helped her reel in her catch.

"He's a big one, muffin. Hold on. We'll get him in together." Carefully guiding the child and adding his strength to hers, he helped her wind the line, bringing her catch closer and closer to shore.

"Here's the net." Jed handed it to Adam, who scooped the fish from the water.

"My fish!" Summer wailed. "It's a turtle."

"Indeed it is, and a big one too. Do you feel like turtle soup tonight instead of trout?"

"Daddy! We can't eat this turtle. It might be somebody's mommy."

"And the fish wouldn't?" Adam cut the line and set it free.

"I hadn't thought of that," Summer admitted. "But anyway, a fish doesn't look as much like a mommy as a turtle does."

Tracy's sputtering laughter joined with Liza's and Jed's. Adam fought the smile that quirked his lips in spite of himself.

"Does your daughter get that sort of logic from her father too?" Tracy asked tongue-in-cheek.

"Heaven help me, I have no idea where that came from," Adam said quietly, so that Summer couldn't hear. "Do you think the mountain has gotten to her as it has her father . . . in a bit of a different way?"

Tracy prudently chose to ignore the remark. "What did you use for bait, Summer?"

"The rest of my peanut butter sandwich."

"Peanut but—" Tracy smothered a smile. "You really should have waited for one of us to bait your hook. You could've gotten a barb in your finger."

"That's all right. I didn't have any trouble. I just squeezed it on."

"Adam," Jed managed to say amid gasps of hilarity, "I

think your daughter has just invented a whole new way to fish. Who knows, maybe next time she'll catch one."

"This is fun," Summer said. "I wish we didn't have to leave tomorrow."

Adam instantly looked at Tracy. She had grown quite pale beneath her tan. The time they had been avoiding thinking about had come. They were faced with the specter that had loomed over these last intense days. Though his schedule had been set from the beginning, Adam and Tracy had futilely denied the inevitable by not speaking of it. Now, with the words of an innocent child, they could pretend no longer, and Adam could feel the hurt he saw in Tracy's eyes.

"Come on, Jed," Liza murmured. "Let's put away the picnic supplies."

Tracy realized in some dim recess of her mind that she and Adam were alone. Summer had returned to building sailboats, and Jed and Liza were making a pretense of being absorbed in repacking the picnic basket. But all Tracy knew was that she was hurting as she had never known she could. Tomorrow Adam would be gone from her life.

"Tracy. Darling. It'll only be for a few weeks." He dried away the tears she hadn't known were falling. "Summer's due in school the next day. I'll stay for a while to be sure she's settled, then I'll be back." Catching her hands in his, he lifted them to his lips and kissed her fingertips. "I'm not fool enough to say the time will pass before we know it."

"Don't!"

"It might be only a week or two." He hated the hopelessness he heard in her single word. "Tracy, Summer needs me."

"I know."

"She's a well-adjusted child. In two weeks or so she should be perfectly attuned to the class. First grade shouldn't be so different from kindergarten. Luckily she knows the teacher. That should help." Adam cursed himself for babbling inanely. There was a deep sadness about Tracy that no words he might offer could wipe away.

"Tracy? I have to go now," Summer said. She was subdued, much of her excitement dimmed. "Jed's going to take Liza and me home."

"I'll walk back to the car with you." Tracy took the child's hand and they followed Jed and Liza toward her cabin. Adam walked behind, aware of how his daughter clung to Tracy.

By the car Tracy knelt before Summer. "I'll miss you. Maybe if you study hard and do well, your daddy will bring you back for a holiday."

"Can we, Daddy?" Summer's solemn eyes pleaded with him.

"I'm sure we can."

"Then give me a kiss," Tracy said, "And I'll see you soon." Summer's pudgy arms wound tightly around her neck and a kiss that was sticky with peanut butter was pressed to her cheek.

"I love you, Tracy."

"And I love you, Summer. Good-bye, Liza, Jed. Come again soon."

Tracy stood perfectly still as Jed's car left her drive. It had gone completely from sight before she faced Adam. "I know you have to go and I'm sorry I've acted such a fool."

"I never meant for it to happen like this. We both know we had to talk about it before the day was over, but I'd hoped to find an easier way."

"Is there an easy way?"

"No." Adam was stricken by the loneliness he could already see in her face. "We still have the rest of this evening."

"Yes. We do." Tracy clasped his hand in hers. Very slowly she led him up the steps and into her cabin.

Nine

There was a sharp rap at the workshop door. Deep in concentration, Tracy frowned but did not consciously acknowledge it. With great care and delicate precision she changed the flow of a line by trimming away a single sliver. The rapping sounded again, this time penetrating her thoughts.

She put down the fragile figure and her tools and rose from her chair. Still looking at the carving that had so engrossed her, she brushed woodchips from her jeans and wiped her hands on a towel hanging from the table.

"Tracy." The muffled call broke the total absorption in her work.

"Coming." Absently pushing aside her unbraided hair, she walked to the door and opened it. "Jed, you're early—Adam!"

"Good morning, Tracy." He straightened from the doorframe, lifted a long curl to his lips, and breathed deeply. "Nice."

She looked up at him in complete surprise, moving only to tuck back the strand of hair he had kissed.

"Your mouth's open, darling." He grinned down at her.

"What're you doing here? You're supposed to be half-way to New York City by now."

"Whatever happened to Good morning Adam. How are you?"

"Oh—uh, yes, well. Good morning, Adam."

"Is this always your early morning voice, or do you just stutter on the odd days?"

Tracy laughed then and relaxed. "I only stutter when I find a man who shouldn't be there standing on my doorstep."

"If I think about it a minute, I might make some sense of that."

"Adam, what are you doing here?" A whimper sounded behind him and Tracy looked past him into the yard. "Is Summer with you? Where's Liza? And Jed? Aren't you going to miss your plane?"

"Taking your questions in order, I'm here to bring you something. No. Gone to the airport. With Liza and Summer. No. There, does that take care of all of them?" He ran his finger down her forehead and tapped her gently on the nose. "If so, then I have a question for you."

"Oh, yeah?" Tracy was so happy to see him that she failed to notice that he didn't say what he had brought her. "And just what question might that be?"

"Well, I was wondering if you were planning to make me stand here all day, or are you going to invite me in?"

"Of course, sir, and welcome to my humble workshop." She stepped from the door and bowed low in flamboyant courtesy. "Won't you have a seat?"

"First things first," he muttered as he drew her into his arms. "Were you going to make me wait all day for this too?"

"No." On tiptoe, Tracy met his kiss eagerly. Her arms locked tightly about his neck, her body molded to his. When his lips met hers, she sighed softly in pleasure.

Reluctantly Adam lifted his head from hers. With one arm still around her he walked her to the work table. "Something new?" he asked, indicating the rough figure on the table.

"Yes. Something to keep me busy while you're away."

"What is it?"

"It's a surprise."

"For me?"

"Yes. It should be ready by the time you return."

Adam only nodded and released her. He prowled the room, looking at her carvings that were scattered about in profusion. "Do you know, even though I've seen these a dozen times, it's always astonishing to see what you can make a block of wood portray. There's too much beauty here for it to be hidden away."

"Thank you, Adam." Tracy knew where this was leading and firmly changed the subject. "Would you like some coffee? It's still warm."

"No, thanks." He accepted defeat, but only for the moment.

Tracy leaned against the table and watched him as he moved from one carving to another. "You still haven't said why you're here."

"You weren't listening, love. I answered that question first. I brought you something." He stepped outside the cabin and returned immediately. "This."

Before she could react he placed a wriggling brown and black ball of fur into her arms.

"What?" Tracy looked blankly at the fuzzy puppy he had given her. "No! Here." She tried to push it back at him. "I don't want this. Take it back!"

"Can't." Adam backed away, refusing to take the dog from her. "He's yours."

"He's not! I don't want another dog."

"Want and need can be two different things."

"Then"—Tracy gritted her teeth—"I don't *need* another dog. There's no place in my life for another one."

"Obviously he thinks differently." Adam grinned as a pink tongue licked Tracy's finger.

"I said no!" She gently set the dog outside. Even in her anger she couldn't bring herself to hurt it by simply dropping it. Before she could straighten, though, the puppy scampered back to her side as quickly as his short legs could carry him.

"Adam, take it away."

"I can't. My plane leaves in less than an hour and I'll have to drive like a bat out of hell to make it now."

"Adam, please take it."

"His name is Bear. Summer thought it fit."

"I won't keep him."

"That's up to you. Where Bear belongs is something the two of you are going to have to settle between you. But it looks as if his decision's made." Adam nodded to the puppy, who was now sleeping contentedly on an extra shirt of Tracy's that had dropped on the floor. "He may not be yours, but he thinks you're his. Now, kiss me again. I have to go."

She had no time for further protest. He swept her into his arms and kissed her thoroughly. As he drew away he said almost sternly, "Remember, I love you, and I'll be back as soon as I can."

Then he was gone. Long after his car had disappeared and the dust had settled, she stared after him, her fingers pressed to her lips. In a pain-filled daze she walked to the front porch steps and sank down on them. With her knees drawn up and her fists clenched, she huddled there.

"Fool," she said aloud. "If it hurts this badly when he leaves for only a short while, how will you survive when he's gone for good?" Tortured by her thoughts, she wasn't aware that tears were streaming down her face until a small, warm body crept into her lap and a rough little tongue started licking her chin.

"Go away. I don't want you." She pushed the dog from her lap.

Bear whimpered, tilted his head curiously, then wagged his stub of a tail with zest. Tracy didn't see his attempt at friendship; her head was buried in her arms as silent sobs shook her. Sensing that something was wrong, but unable to understand what, the puppy crept as close to her as he could. He was still there when she rose. She returned to her workshop and shut the door firmly in his face.

Tracy had no idea how long the scratching had been going on, for she had been involved in a particularly tedious part of her carving. At such times she could easily block everything but the figure before her from her mind. Now that she was satisfied with her accomplishment, she was again aware of her surroundings. Once she noticed the sound, she found it impossible to ignore. Angrily tossing her knife on the table, she pushed back her chair and went to the door. Throwing it open, she glared down at the dog.

"Now, look. I've given you food and water. You're not ill; you have a place to sleep. There's nothing more I can give you. I know you're lonesome, but I can't let you in here. I don't want you to get attached to me because as soon as I have time I'm going to find you a home."

Bear only looked up at her, thumped his tail, and Tracy could have sworn he smiled.

"Don't you ply your charms on me. It won't do you a bit of good. As soon as possible, you're leaving. That's final." Again she shut the door, blocking out his wistful expression.

For nearly a week it had been the same. Tracy saw to his needs, promised herself that soon she would find him a home, then firmly shut herself away from him.

"What now?" Tracy tossed aside her brush, closed up the pot of paint, and stalked to the door. The incessant barking had been a minor irritant for the past ten minutes. Now there was a shrill, urgent quality about it that she could no longer ignore.

As she crossed the yard, seeking the source of her trouble and meaning to scold him severely, she heard the sound that no one from the valley could mistake—the angry, rapid buzzing of a rattlesnake. It was followed by a soft thump and a yelp from Bear. After a split-second, the buzzing resumed.

Tracy knew what she would see before she rounded the corner of her cabin. Bear had discovered a rattler. It had struck and recoiled again, but had it found its mark? Bear's barking was little assurance, for she knew he might be staggering and ill in a matter of minutes.

She stopped short, fear roiling in the pit of her stomach. On her porch, its tail high, its rattles moving faster than the eye could follow, and its head drawn back prepared to strike again, was one of the largest snakes she had ever seen. Bear was dancing and prancing just beyond its reach, his shrill bark sliding into bass now and then. He teased the snake with all the enthusiasm of a playful puppy.

Her first instinct was to call out, but common sense told her that to distract him could bring disaster. Her hand went by habit to the knife at her belt. To get a clear target, she knew she would have to circle behind Bear, hoping that she wouldn't draw his attention.

So began one of the most agonizing journeys Tracy had ever taken. Carefully placing one foot in front of the other, she edged her way through the yard. Every move was slow and calculated. Once again the snake struck and Bear danced out of its range. Tracy had to force herself not to scream her warning. Beads of perspiration were on her forehead, and her cheeks were flushed by the time she had come half circle to the other side of the cabin. Praying that Bear would not make an unexpected move, she drew back the knife, aimed, and threw it with all her strength.

For one long, anguished moment, she thought she had missed. The rattling grew even angrier, rising to a fevered pitch, then abruptly ceased. She couldn't look. Sinking down on the grass, she buried her face in her hands. Her whole body was trembling from the tension.

The grass whispered and the patter of feet stopped. She knew he was there waiting. She lifted her head and looked into golden-brown eyes. "Okay, mutt, you win."

Bear's body seemed to vibrate with love at the sound of her voice, but still he didn't move.

"Well, don't be shy at this late date." Tracy laughed and pulled him into her lap. Bear snuggled closer, burrowed his nose into her hair, and with a gusty sigh relaxed against her. "So you're going to be a lover, are you? Before you get too comfortable, let me look at you."

She held the pup from her and truly looked at him for the first time. "Now, let's see just exactly what you are. Airedale? Maybe some collie and even hound? You are a mutt, did you know?" She shook him playfully and was rewarded with a wet kiss.

"Now I know you're an airedale, and exactly like your father. Noah Hawkins's Rebel is the biggest lover in the valley, and you look and act just like him. I wonder who he visited this time? What staid and proper lady dog did he woo then leave with his little bastards?" Bear barked at that. "Sorry, didn't mean to hurt your feelings.

"Adam was right, you seem to have chosen me and there's not a thing I can do about it. So, since it's to be you and I, suppose we both go attend to an unpleasant matter."

Pushing Bear off her lap, she stood and for the first time looked at the dead snake. A shiver ran through her when she remembered how the pup had cornered it. She looked down at him. "Bear, I believe you have more courage than you have sense. Come on. There's no need in putting it off. We have a snake to dispose of."

Tracy looked up and smiled as Bear stirred restlessly and growled. "Something out there interests you, does it? Just make sure you don't find any more rattlesnakes. One was more than enough."

Bear rose and wagged his whole body as he was prone

to do when she spoke to him in such a teasing way. She laughed, rubbed his ears, and pushed him toward the door. "Go on. You might as well investigate. You won't be happy until you do."

She smiled indulgently as he slipped and stumbled over his own feet in his haste to leave. With her back to the open door, Tracy resumed the last of the painting of the exquisite carving. She always worked now with the door open so Bear could come and go as he wished, though he very seldom strayed from her side. There must have been something of great interest out there, Tracy thought as she again became immersed in the painting.

When she heard him return, she didn't bother to look up. "That didn't take long."

"That's strange. I thought it took forever."

"Adam!" She dropped her brush, spattering paint on her shirt. Her chair fell with a crash as she leaped up to face him.

He stood in the doorway, the reality of her love. His tie was loose and his shirt-sleeves rolled up. The navy blazer hung from a crooked finger across his shoulder. With the sun behind him he was a shadowy figure, but to Tracy he was the light of her day. Her throat was dry, her lips parched, and her feet seemed to be nailed to the floor.

"If I can come nonstop all the way from New York, do you think the woman in my life could cross the room for me?"

"Adam! I thought you'd never come." Tracy was in his arms before she finished speaking. When his lips met hers, with his short-clipped and luxuriant beard brushing her face, it was as if her life had begun again.

Adam wound her flowing hair about his hands as he drew away. "How have you been?" he asked, his voice a husky whisper.

"Lonely."

"Have you been working too hard?"

"Not really." She searched his face intently, seeing an underlying strain. She frowned in concern. "Are you ill?"

"Only tired. I've been busier than I expected."

"Adam! Is something wrong? Is it Summer or Liza."

"No, they're both fine. There were some technical problems about the book. Most of them have been worked out."

"Most, but not all?"

"I'm afraid not." He rested his weary head against her hair.

"Then you shouldn't be here. You should've stayed where you needed to be."

"Tracy, this *is* the place I most need to be. You wouldn't believe how I've missed you. I couldn't work for thinking of you. So I—what the hell!"

They both heard the ferocious growl just before Adam's shoe was attacked. Never one to be left out of anything, Bear chose this method to join in. Adam bent to look him in the eye.

"And just who do you think you are to interrupt when I finally have my woman in my arms? Hasn't anyone taught you that it's bad manners?"

"You're now looking at my other shadow," Tracy said, grinning. "Don't look at me like that; he was your idea."

"But"—Adam rose and took her back into his arms—"he was to keep you company when I was gone, not while I'm here."

"Tell him that . . . and lots of luck. You said Bear had decided I was his and you were right."

"Maybe I'd best try to find him a lady of his own."

"I think he's a bit too young just yet. But if his father's who I think he is, he won't need your help."

"Hester Calton had him. She said something about Noah Hawkins's Rebel had been visiting."

"That's what I thought. Rebel gets around. You can see his mark on more than half the young dogs in the valley."

Bear barked and wagged his tail.

"Go find your own girl. This one's mine," Adam said, then laughed when the puppy wagged everything. "He's enthusiastic, to say the least."

Even though he laughed and teased, Tracy could see the fatigue in the deep creases around Adam's mouth. "Have you had your dinner?"

"It was served on the plane, but I was working and didn't eat."

"I have some spaghetti on the stove, and a salad. Would you like some?"

"That sounds like heaven. I've been so eager to get back here that even before I left I skipped a meal or two and stayed at my desk."

"Then why don't you go on to the house and wash up? I'll be there in a minute."

"You won't be long?" His eyes seemed hungry for more of her.

"No, I'll only be a minute. I promise."

"I'll hold you to that. Only a minute."

The last of the dishes were done; the kitchen was all in order. Adam leaned against the counter with a glass of wine in his hand, watching Tracy put away the last pieces of silverware.

"That was the best meal I've had in a long time," he said.

"I'm glad you liked it."

"I really should be going." He set his glass on the counter.

"Have you been back to your cabin?" Tracy concentrated fiercely on the flowers she was rearranging in a small vase.

"I came straight to you, Tracy, but now I suppose I'd better go along."

"Don't go." Her trembling voice hardly rose above a whisper.

"Tracy?" Adam was afraid to trust himself, afraid that he had heard only what he wanted to hear.

"I asked you not to go." She turned to face him, her eyes were wide with desire. "Stay with me. I need you."

"You need me?" He pulled her to him with an urgency that was almost painful. "Do you know how I've ached for you? I've been trying all evening to think of some way to ask you if I could stay here with you. Then you look at me so honestly and cut right to the heart of the matter in the most enchanting way."

"Where else would I want you to be, Adam?" she asked matter-of-factly. "Why don't you get your bag from the car while I see to Bear? I'll put a fresh towel in the spare bath for you."

While he was gone, Tracy readied the bathroom for him. She laid out a towel and fresh soap, and the grooming kit she had bought for him. She had no idea how he cared for his beard and mustache, but hopefully anything he might need would be there. Before he returned she was back in the kitchen.

"Did you say the spare bath?" he asked.

"Yes. Then you won't have to fight my clutter."

"Okay, but I wouldn't mind clutter that was yours."

"That's what you think. You haven't been slapped in the face with drying 'unmentionables.' "

"I look forward to the day," he said, laughing as he walked down the hall to the assigned bath.

Tracy busied herself in the kitchen, fussing over nothing. She gave Bear his supper and saw that he was settled for the night. It wasn't until she heard the water running that she made her way to her own bath.

Tracy stepped from the shower, dried herself vigorously, then slipped the ribbon from her hair. From her closet she took a sheer robe that fastened at the waist with a satin belt. She slipped her arms into it, belted it tightly, then crossed the carpeted floor to her dressing table. First she applied a touch of fragrance to her earlobes, the hollow of her throat, and the cleft between her breasts. Next she began to brush her heavy mane of hair. Lost in her memories of Adam and how he had looked today, she did not hear his quiet tread. It wasn't until he took the brush from her hand that she saw his image in the mirror.

In a short navy robe, water glistening in his hair, he was an image of contrasts, dark and light. When he set the brush on the dresser and offered her his hand, Tracy did not demur. She let him lift her from the chair and waited while his eyes traveled over her as if seeing her body for the first time.

He untied the sash slowly. The harsh sound of his indrawn breath broke the silence of the room. The sheer fabric swung open to reveal the shadowy valley between her breasts and the inner flesh of one thigh.

Tracy waited, calm beneath his adoring gaze. When his rough hands rasped against her bare shoulders, she did not move. Gently Adam slipped the robe from her, letting it fall neglected to the floor.

Only then did she touch him. With a strange calm she untied his own belt and, moving nearer, pushed the robe from his shoulders. Her memory had been faithful, for he was beautiful.

"This is the moment I've dreamed of for days," he whispered as he took both her hands in his. "There were times when I could almost feel your touch." He turned to the quilt-covered bed, swept back the blankets, turned off the lamp on the night table, and all was in darkness.

Lightning flashed in the sky. Thunder answered in a low, deep rumble over mountaintops and through the low-hanging clouds. One minute all was an empty black, then a blue-white blaze bathed every object, every shadow in an eerie glow. This was the world outside Tracy's cabin. A symphony of sound surrounded them, muted by the steady drone of rain beating down on the tin roof, giving back a soft melody of its own.

The two who lay curled amid the covers of the massive antique bed found a responsive chord in the storm. Their arms were entwined, Tracy's head was pillowed on Adam's shoulder, and his hand curled possessively at her hip. The storm was little more that an overt expression of what they had shared.

The gentle rain that had been left by the dying furor was also like this time together. The startling roar of electric excitement, the wild fury, and the sweet, quiet gentleness had all been theirs.

Passion had come to them with little warning, its ferocity and intensity a consuming thing. It had unleashed a wild, primitive love that knew no conventional bounds. Only two who loved equally could have withstood its force, with neither absorbing nor destroying the other.

Each had met the fierceness of the other with a matching spirit, the wildness with a tender savagery, the sweet and the quiet with a gentleness that held no less passion than the first. It had been the rejoining of two who loved and who had found being separate beyond bearing.

Inch by inch, moving with an agonizing care, Tracy slid from the bed. Her robe lay in a tangle on the braided rug. She slipped into it and belted it securely, then glided on bare feet across the floor. A moonbeam caught her in its web, turning the silk to a bright iridescence. For long, quiet moments she stared out at the familiar shape that always loomed before her.

Shadow—benevolent and jealous. Which was it to be with her? As though searching for an answer, she watched the moon cast its glow over the dark mountain.

Adam stirred in his sleep, his arm seeking her giving warmth. With no more thought to her silent question,

Tracy dropped the robe to the floor and slipped quickly into the bed. Her only desire was to be where Adam needed her—at least while she could.

He drew her hard against him, holding her as though he felt threatened.

"Tracy," he muttered as he bound her to him with her hair, his lips resting against the scar. Soon his breathing settled to a soft, easy rhythm as, even in sleep, he drew contentment from her.

Finally Tracy slept for what little of the night was left.

"What was that?" Adam sat upright, realizing that he was alone as he pushed the covers from his body. He was unmindful of his complete—and to Tracy totally beautiful—nakedness.

"That, my beloved, was Livingston, my own personal, dependable alarm clock. What—"

"Say that again!" Adam's voice held the huskiness of sleep and more.

"That was Livingston, a rooster who thinks—"

"No! Not that. The first part."

"Let's see. What was it I said?" Tracy crossed one bare foot over the other and leaned against the doorframe, her head cocked in a pretense of thought. "If it wasn't about Livingston and it wasn't about alarm clocks, what could it be?"

"Tracy!" A playful menace laced his words.

"Ah-ha!" She launched herself at him. "I suddenly remember." From her place, cradled so protectively in his arms, she stroked the short, silken beard. Her voice sank to a loving whisper. "You are my beloved."

"Oh, God." An unusual light shimmered in his eyes as he kissed her forehead. "Only you could make or destroy me with a single word. Beloved. Who would have thought such an old-fashioned word could be the key to the world of my dreams? Say it again, Tracy. Please."

"Beloved Adam. *My* beloved." Her dark eyes shone with a glow he had come to recognize.

His hand stole beneath the loose fabric of her sweatshirt, finding and caressing her bare breasts. "Surely we aren't backpacking today after this rain," he teased.

"Not unless you'd like to experience a mud slide or two firsthand."

"Then why this?" His hands again stroked her breasts and teased the rising nipples.

"I thought . . . I . . ." She blushed furiously.

"That we might make love? Did you leave your body bare so that I might touch you like this?" His fingertips drew from her a shiver of delight. "Don't be ashamed of wanting me, darling. Don't you know that the greatest compliment you could pay me is to want me as much as I want you?"

"Am I that obvious?"

"Only to me, thank God." He drew her farther into his embrace.

She snuggled against him, reveling in his caress. Her fingers curled into the thick hair of his chest as she rested there contentedly. After a while she drew away and stared solemnly into his eyes.

"Adam?"

"Mmm?"

"We have a problem."

"We do?"

"I'm afraid so."

"What is it, love?"

"Your breakfast is burning."

"My what is what?" Adam's mind was clearly not on breakfast.

"Your breakfast. It's burning." She bounded off the bed and was out the door as his laughter rose.

The day was a comfortable one. They built a fire in the old grate to ward off the chill of the early fall day.

Adam sat on the sofa, his papers scattered about him, his pad on his knee. In frowning concentration he composed, destroyed, then recomposed the text that would accompany the photographs of Shadow.

Tracy was hunched over a small table in the corner, her back to Adam and the fire, with Bear at her side. At each crumpled page and the colorful expletives, she smiled but did not halt in her work. Bear only raised a lazy eye as if to say, what now?

"Dammit it all to hell and back again!"

Only Tracy's rollicking laughter and Bear's puzzled thump of his stubby tail followed yet another rattle of crumpling paper.

"Don't laugh," Adam said, looking balefully at her. "It isn't funny. I have all this material that promises to be a marvelous story and it *won't* come together." He stared at the fire. "No matter how I try, it's flat! I can't make it come to life. Somewhere down the line I haven't captured the essence of it. Tracy, I want those who read this to see and to feel the mountain as a . . . a . . . a living thing."

"Perhaps tomorrow when the roads are clear we can begin our research among the old people. Some of them have actually lived a part of the legends. Talking to those who know firsthand should help," Tracy said hopefully.

"Maybe you're right." Adam's fingers stabbed repeatedly through his hair, making it more untidy. "It would probably be best just to put it away for now. I'm certainly making no headway."

"A sensible idea," Tracy murmured, then returned to her own task.

Adam began to straighten his work into some semblance of order, then sat watching the flames. Bear left his place by Tracy to go to him. He leaned heavily against Adam's knee, signaling that he had been neglected long enough and should have his head scratched.

"Spoiled mutt." Adam chuckled as he did as he was required. "I think this should be your lady's job, except she does look a mite busy." He chuckled again, delighted with his own use of one of the local idioms. "Let's find out what it is that keeps her from sharing our laziness. A good idea? I thought so."

Adam turned again to face Tracy. "In case you missed that brilliant one-sided conversation and need an interpretation, darlin', we two lonely males need your company. What could be keeping you from our irresistible presence?"

"Not a thing." Tracy rose, holding the finished carving behind her back. She walked across the room to stand before him. "In fact, I was only waiting until you finished with your work to give you something."

"What?" He looked up at her curiously.

"This." She set the figurine on the table at his side.

"Dear God."

Tracy had heard many harsh words tumble from his lips in his growing frustration, but these were a reverent prayer. He said nothing more, only looked at the carving through eyes that glittered.

In the flicker of the firelight, the tiny figure of mother and child seemed to take on a life of its own. The mother, her blond and fragile head bent over the golden ringlets of the child, throbbed with a vibrant love. Only a fool would not know that a contented child was being sweetly sung to sleep.

"Summer and Sharon." He could hardly say the names. "How did you know? How could you?"

"You told me the first day we met."

"Yes. I remember now." He never took his gaze from the figures. "I told you how Summer loved to be sung to sleep, but not since Sharon died."

"Sharon had a lovely voice."

Adam took a deep breath and looked up at Tracy. "This is beautiful, but I've never known you to carve people."

"I never had until now."

"Why this time?"

"Because you've given me so much. I wanted to give you something in return."

"You've given me far more." Adam lifted her hand to his mouth and kissed each fingertip lingeringly. "You've given me my daughter's life, and my own."

"No . . ."

"Shh." With a gentle tug he drew her down to his lap. "Summer would've died on Shadow if not for you, and for Wolfe. And I would have died with her. Perhaps not physically, but life without meaning is a sort of death."

"Then I'm doubly glad I found her." She settled comfortably into the curve of his shoulder.

As the fire danced, casting its warmth into every corner, they retreated into their thoughts, remembering a woman with hair like new gold and a smile just as bright. Adam was the first to stir as he pulled Tracy nearer his heart.

"We need to speak of Sharon, darling."

"I know."

Quiet hovered again in the room. Neither knew where to start. A coal popped and hissed. At his place near the hearth Bear whimpered and growled, playing some fierce game in his puppy dream. In the light the carved figures seemed to live.

Adam's voice at last broke the silence, rippling through it, deep timbred yet steady. "When we met and fell in love, Sharon was the perfect woman for me. Her soothing calm was the foil for my pent-up restlessness, and I loved her so completely it was frightening. Even when we made love I had to hold a part of myself in check. She wouldn't have understood any but the gentlest love. Had she lived, it would have been enough.

"But the man her death created, the man I am today, must have more. I need the fire and excitement you bring to me. Each of us loved her in our own way. Our lives have been enriched by her short time with us, and I'd like to keep her memory alive for Summer." He picked up the carving and caressed the blond heads lovingly, then set it back down. "But for us, I'd like to put her to rest."

Tracy murmured something indistinguishable and turned her face into his shirt.

"I'll always love her memory," he continued. "It's something precious and inviolate, but still only a memory. A new Adam has risen from the ashes and pain of her death. A richer, wiser, and a far stronger Adam. I love you, Tracy."

She lifted her head to gaze into his eyes. "I know," she said, her hand stroking his cheek at the line of his beard. "I understand, but you needn't worry. I have no guilt about Sharon. Instead I think that wherever she is, she's happy that we had this time together."

"I think you're right. Sharon would like her best fellow and best friend to find a love together. She was an incurable matchmaker. If you hadn't . . ."

"If I hadn't had the accident," she supplied. "It's all right, Adam. That should also be put to rest. We both need to lock those closets and throw away the key." She straightened abruptly. "Now, what sort of matchmaking did Sharon have in mind for me? Was he handsome? Devilishly charming? A lady-killer? Hmm, on second thought, he doesn't sound half bad. You wouldn't happen to still have his phone number, would you? I have use of a good man around here every now and then."

"Oh, you do, do you?" The gleam in his eye warned her.

"No, Adam, no. You wouldn't. You know I'm ticklish."

"Oh, wouldn't I?" His imitation of a wicked leer threw her further into fits of merriment. "Just watch."

"No! Oh, no. Please. My grandfather always warned me to remain a mystery. Never to let a man know my weaknesses or my secrets."

"Ah, but you did, and I do. So what will you do about it?"

"Anything, anything. Just don't tickle me."

"Did I hear the lady cry uncle?"

"Uncle. Uncle."

"Who is it that needs a man?"

"I do."

"And who is that man?"

"You, Adam, only you."

"Prove it."

"Like this?" A tiny kiss grazed his cheek.

"Another."

"This?" The second lingered deliciously on his lips.

"You're getting the hang of it."

"Shall I try again?"

"Practice makes perfect."

"Then never let it be said I didn't strive for perfection."

Bear had watched this human game with a puppy's interest. Now he cocked his head at the sudden silence. After a moment he laid his head between his paws and returned to the field of clover, where rabbits played in abundance.

"Adam, I love you."

"I know, love, I know."

Only the sounds of the fire and the soft sighs of the sleeping dog were heard for a long time.

Ten

"Are you sure?"

"Positive."

"How can you be so positive?"

"Because I'm *positive!*"

"Tell me how."

"Look, Adam." Tracy leaned against the jeep, struggling to hide her grin. "We aren't going to get stuck and you're not going to have to walk out of some deep, dank quagmire. The water runs off these hills in a hurry. You are familiar with their slight slope, I hope."

"Slight slope?" Adam grinned at her marvelous understatement.

"Come on," she said, "hop in the jeep. We're wasting most of the morning with this chit-chat."

"Chit-chat she calls it. All right," Adam grumbled as he climbed over the dented door. "*But* I'm not above saying I told you so if we get stuck."

"Good." Tracy put the jeep in gear and moved slowly out of the rutted drive. "You can tell me with every stroke while you're digging us out of your anticipated mud hole."

"We'll see," he said, still unconvinced. "Who's first?"

It was the sort of day Tracy had predicted. The visits were many, the tales fascinating, the food plentiful and delicious, and the host always reluctant to let them go. At day's end they were greeted by a lonely Bear and were as glad to be home as he was to see them. There was no pretense that Adam should stay anywhere but with Tracy.

In the early pre-dawn hours Tracy stood alone before the window, staring silently at the moonlit Shadow.

"Okay. You've made a believer of me. I won't argue *anything*," Adam said. Dressed in jeans and a heavy sweater, he was standing by the jeep, ready for the day's excursion.

"I'll believe that when I don't see it." This sort of badinage had become commonplace between them, as natural as breathing.

"There's not one steep incline, one deep gulley, or one sheer drop that's going to worry me. *And* I refuse to turn my head into a punching bag today. You drive. I'll relax."

"Terrific. Except today's different. We're going to the other side of the valley to visit the only Indian family that still has a farm here."

"Across the valley?"

"Yep."

"Across the *flat* valley?"

"Very flat."

Adam sighed. "Then, in that case, I'll drive."

"Revenge?"

"No, love. Just reasserting my bruised male ego."

"Show me the bruise, I'll kiss it well."

"Ah, but then we wouldn't make today's visit." He held out his hand for the keys.

"Spoil-sport!" Tracy laughed and dropped them into his waiting grasp.

* * *

Jimmy Black Hawk's family was a large one, spanning four generations. It was a true blending of the old and the new, and each member of the family had his or her own contribution about the legend of the waterfall. After they had waved good-bye and promised to visit again soon, Adam drove back to Tracy's, not speaking.

"What are you thinking, Adam?" Tracy's soft question drew him back to the present.

"That you were right. The legend about Indian Maid Fall is beautiful. Until I heard Jimmy describing it, I hadn't realized how dangerous internal strife could be for the Indian tribes."

She nodded her agreement. "They had troubles enough without fighting among themselves."

"If those two young people hadn't met at the fall, and if their love hadn't been strong enough to overcome their differences, there might never have been peace."

"The entire tribe could easily have been decimated. Then there would've been no beautiful Black Hawk family," Tracy added.

"They are a handsome people, aren't they? I wonder if the lovers were as handsome."

"Does it matter?"

"No." Adam glanced at her. "It doesn't matter at all. But such a strong love had to make them proud and beautiful."

"Yes," Tracy said. "Proud and very beautiful."

The days passed far too quickly. With each visit, Adam added to his store of knowledge. With each conversation he learned and understood more and more about the legends. He learned how each had come to be, how they had been kept alive, and how they had been protected. No one had been reticent about speaking with him. It was as if he bore Tracy's stamp of approval, and that was enough.

The day arrived, as they knew it must, when all the

visits had been made but one. Tracy had deliberately saved it for last. It was the legend that was most special to her.

"Is Opal expecting us?" Adam asked her.

"Yes. I told Noah Hawkins that we'd be over that way at the first of this week. Opal has no telephone, but the grapevine's a wonderful thing. I wonder if smoke signals could've been any quicker."

"From what I've seen, I doubt it."

They were quiet for the remainder of the long, rough drive. The day was lovely, but for Tracy it held a touch of sadness. Soon there would be no reason for Adam to remain in the valley. Already the dread of the coming confrontation was chilling her heart.

A gaggle of geese greeted them as they drove into the yard of the tiniest cabin Adam had seen yet.

"It is small, isn't it?" Tracy said, reading his thoughts. "Opal feels more secure in small areas."

"Because of her blindness?"

"She's never said, but I think it's probably so." She swung down from the jeep and waited while he did the same. "If you're wondering about the geese, they're her watchdogs."

"Watchdogs!" Then remembering the furor they had caused, he understood. "I can see very well where they would be excellent for the job."

"Why don't you sit here on the porch? I'll go inside and bring her out. She loves to feel the sunlight on her face."

When Tracy returned, the old woman clung to her arm as she walked to a battered rocker.

"Good day, young man," she said once she was seated.

"How are you, Opal?"

"Tolerable, just tolerable. Tracy says you want to ask about Dougal MacLaren."

"I've seen his cave and I'd like to know more about him, and his Laura."

"I don't know much of the MacLaren hisself, but I know a mite about the clan. They took to being soldiers for pay and 'tis that answer I favor for the MacLaren. Why else would he be in this country, and why else marked so terrible?

"I know naught of his Laura. None ever know'd her beginnings or why she was lost and alone in the snow. The best I know of my mother and father is that theirs was a great love. It could span all earth and time."

Opal's blank gaze fixed itself on Adam's face. For a disconcerting moment he forgot she couldn't see. "Have you heard the MacLaren's pipes yet, lad?"

"No." Adam was curious. In all that had been said about the MacLaren and his legend, no one had mentioned that the pipes might still be heard. "When would I hear them, Opal? Would it be on the mountain, or near the cave?"

"It could be, but you can hear them anywhere. On the mountain, in the valley. Where you are don't matter. It's who you're with that counts."

"I couldn't hear the pipes alone?"

"No. You only hear them when you're with your last and true love."

"Have you heard them, Opal?" Adam asked softly.

"Aye, but not for a long spell. Not since my Joshua died."

"Do you think I'll hear them?"

"You're a stubborn flatlander and you refuse the believing of our legends, but you will believe . . . and someday you'll hear the pipes." Opal grew silent. It was obvious that this short talk had taxed her strength.

"You're tired," Tracy said. She had remained standing by the rocker. "Let me take you back inside."

"No. Thank you, but I think I'll sit a time in the sun." Her wrinkled old hand patted Tracy's as it rested on her shoulder. "You and yore young man go on along. Harvey will be from the field soon. I'll go in then."

"You'll be all right?"

"Of course. Take yore man and go. But Tracy, I'll look to be seeing you again real soon."

"I'll be here." Tracy kissed Opal's withered cheek, then walked back to the jeep with Adam.

They spent the rest of the day rambling over the trails of Shadow. It was nearly dark before they returned to Tracy's cabin. Dinner was quiet, both subdued by the realization that an interlude had come to an end. Adam's research was complete. It was time that he moved on.

Their loving that night was an untamed and all-consuming thing. Amid their soft whispers they spoke with their bodies and hearts. They were lovers who could drink from the well, but they had a thirst that could never be slaked. Dawn had begun to lighten the sky before their needs were momentarily fulfilled.

Adam woke slowly. He knew that Tracy wasn't with him, and he instinctively looked to the window. She stood there, wrapped in a quilt, staring up at Shadow.

"Good morning, love."

"Adam! I didn't know you were awake." She turned to him.

"I haven't been for long." He saw the sad, serious look on her face. "What are you thinking, Tracy?"

"That you'll be leaving soon."

"Yes, and I'll miss the mountain and the valley." He shifted the pillows behind him in order to sit erect. "I thought I'd spend a few days at the shore getting the material in sequence before I try to write the actual copy. Summer's so excited. She has it all planned out. When I told her that this time when I came home you'd be with me, she was beside herself. I—" Adam stopped short, startled by the sudden pallor on Tracy's face.

"Damn my impatient tongue!" he said, his voice filled with irritation. He got out of the bed and walked over to her. With his hands on her shoulders he drew her near.

"I'm sorry, darling. I meant to wait to do this with a bit more style. Flowers, candlelight, soft music, and even bended knee." His rueful laugh flowed over her. He started to speak again, but stopped when he saw the shattered look on her face. His gaze traveled over her, seeking the softness he had come to love.

Tracy turned and fled from his touch, taking refuge in the huge bed, the place of her happiest moments. She was lovely there in the tangled covers, with her hair tumbling about her shoulders and the quilt clutched to her bare breasts. The knuckles of her right hand were white with strain, and the hand shook with a barely noticeable tremor. Her eyes were dull, fathomless pits—too deep for any light to reach their darkness.

Pain like none he had ever known clutched at Adam, banding his heart with the cold of bitter premonition. He turned away to stare out the window. Drawing a shallow breath, he forced a calmness into his voice that hid the shock that ravaged him.

"You're not going with me, are you, Tracy? You're not going to marry me."

"No."

"Why?" He couldn't turn, couldn't face what he might see. "Have you decided that you don't love me after all?"

"Yes." She tried to lie, but seeing the flinching of the muscles in his taut back, she found she couldn't. "No!" Her voice sank to a soft urgent whisper. "You know I love you."

"Then why? For God's sake, tell me why!"

"I can't go with you because I can't function in your world." Beneath the flat, blunt statement lurked a plea for understanding, but Adam didn't hear it.

"Dammit, Tracy." He turned to her, his face a desolate mask. "It wouldn't be *my* world. It's *ours*."

Tracy sat as she was, unmoving, yet stricken by the powerful longing to take him in her arms and smooth away the slashing furrows by his mouth. Somewhere in the deepest well of her soul her own pain blended with his, promising her a living hell. But because she loved him, she had to send him away.

"Adam." That love trembled in the sound of her voice, his name becoming an endearment. "It could never be our world. I thought it could be. I dreamed it. I wished it. I willed it, but . . . it can never be."

She looked away, unable to bear the despair in his empty eyes. From the window she could see Shadow looming. Shadow, the massive and powerful force that had shaped her life, was her destiny. Her own eyes were bleak when they met and held his. "This is my world, Adam. My only world."

"Then I'll come back to Shadow. If you can't share what you consider mine, I'll share yours. We'll build something together here."

"It wouldn't work." She shook her head in despair. "You have your own obligations to meet. Your photography, Summer—"

"Summer can be a part of our lives no matter where we are," he interrupted harshly, then added softly, "She loves you."

"I know, and I love her." Now the pain rose from that dark, hidden place, cutting like broken glass through her voice. A stray strand of white hair fell against her cheek as she dropped her head and stared blindly at the ancient pattern of the quilt. "I love you both. That's why I can't tie you to me. What kind of lives could you have, either of you, hidden away here with an emotional cripple? I can't . . . I won't let you live your lives half in the real world, half with me."

"And if we want to?"

"No! You both lost so much when Sharon died, yet you've built lives that are vibrant and full of meaning. I can't let you throw that away." She lifted her head. The dull, dry eyes now glistened with gathering tears.

Adam wanted to hold her, to still her trembling lips with his own. He wanted to quiet the pain-filled, probing words. But he didn't dare. Her control was too tenuous, the break too near. How could he explain that without her there would be existence, but not life? Yet had he the power to explain, she wouldn't listen. He said nothing.

"You were happy before you came to Shadow, weren't you, Adam?"

"Yes."

"Then you will be again."

No! Never again. Not without you.

"Between the three of you, you and Liza and Marjorie have made Summer into a beautiful, well-adjusted child. She'll forget me in time, just as you must. It's best we let this be our last good-bye."

"No!" The word was ripped from his aching throat.

"Please don't make this more difficult than it is already. If you'll only listen to me, you'll know I'm right." Her gaze faltered and she looked again at Shadow. "I can't ask you to live scurrying from one place to another, from one agonizing good-bye to another. Each of us would be hurting, opening and reopening the wounds of loss until neither of us would see the other as anything but a source of torment."

He made a low sound of pain and disbelief, and she looked up at him. Her face reflected her own pain. "How could either of us live with the uncertainty?" she said. "You with never knowing what you would find each time you return—love or hate. And me wondering which time you'd find you couldn't face another good-bye." Her voice throbbed with a muted and distant sorrow, as if she were already in that far and desolate future. Adam had to bend near to hear her whisper, "Which time wouldn't you return?"

"It wouldn't have to be like that, darling," he said. "Others live very separate lives, yet together."

"Could we? Wouldn't we spend our time together dreading our next parting? How long would it be before that overshadowed any joy we might find?"

"You love me, Tracy."

"Yes!" The word was a vehement profession of what Adam had never doubted.

"Yet not enough to come with me. Not enough to leave Shadow."

"I can't! Adam, I can't!" Tears spilled over her cheeks, looking like liquid opals against the chalky hue of her skin.

"And if there should be a child?"

"Oh, God!" Tracy bent nearly double, her arms clutching her abdomen. "I must've been mad."

"What if there's a child, Tracy?" Adam prodded, but gently, kindly.

"There is no child, Adam. I'm sure."

"Not from the mountain, perhaps, but what about now? What about this very minute? The fruit of last night could be growing in your body even as we speak."

"No. There's no child. The timing's wrong." This lie she let stand as a fervid yearning was born.

"My poor darling." Adam sat on the bed and drew her into his arms. "This has all happened too fast. You're frightened and confused."

His hand found its way under her heavy hair. Gentle fingers soothed the tense muscles of her neck. "We've shared too much in too little time. You're still off balance and reeling from the shock of it all.

"You've come from a world of careful words and calculated moves to one of abandon in one fell swoop." He brushed a tangled lock from her shoulder, then smoothed it down her back. "It's a new world for you, with new emotions and new love. In the past you lost everyone you ever loved. Now you're sending me away before you get hurt again." His voice broke and dropped to a deeper note. "It's too late, darling. Far too late."

A shake of her head drew a patient sigh from him. Tenderly he held her unresisting body closer.

"What you don't realize is that all the partings in the world could never hurt as much as a final farewell, the one that would mean we'd never see each other again. A hundred good-byes, a million, none would matter as long as they were followed by one more loving hello. I'd never like being apart from you, Tracy, but knowing I'd soon be seeing you would make each separation bearable."

"You're wrong! It would destroy us. You'd come to hate me for tying you to the mountain, for interrupting your life with my insecurities."

"Only losing each other could destroy us, darling."

"Adam . . ."

"Shh." He tilted her chin up and kissed each eyelid. "I won't argue or push. All I can do is prove my point." He stood abruptly and crossed the room. With his back to the window, blocking Shadow from her view, he absorbed the picture of her heartbreaking confusion.

"I'll leave today. I'm not due back in New York until later in the week, but if I go now, I can sneak in an extra day or two with Summer."

Tracy's heart shattered. He was going away. It was exactly what she wanted, what she had convinced herself was best. Yet it still hurt.

"I'll catch an afternoon plane." He walked back to the bed again and looked down at her. With a compelling hand he lifted her chin. "Six months from now, on the first day of spring, I'll be on the first plane back. Then if you still feel the same, if you still want me to go, I'll step out of your life."

He leaned to kiss her. "If I'm going to make that plane, I'd better grab a shower and pack."

Before Tracy could think of a sensible response he was gone. Soon the wonderfully familiar sound of his off-key whistle blended with the drone of running water. It was more than she could stand. Slipping quickly from the bed, she dressed in jeans and a shirt, then hurried from the house, seeking shelter and comfort in her workshop.

*   *   *

Nearly an hour later, as she sat staring blankly at the virgin block of wood, she heard his footsteps on the porch. Her hands gripped her knife so tightly, the handle itself threatened to harm her.

"Tracy."

She made no response. Only the tensing of her body showed that she had heard.

"Darling, it's time."

She faced him then. He was standing just inside the room dressed in the navy blazer that enhanced the silver of his hair and the dignity of his carriage. He was, indeed, a man of great attraction, if not true beauty. There were so many pictures of him that she would carry in her heart, and this was another.

"My plane leaves in just under two hours."

"That soon?" It was a soft question that fooled neither one with its calmness.

"Yes. It seemed best to get on home. I know you hate good-byes, but I couldn't leave without saying it." He moved easily through the room and lifted her from the chair. His kiss was warm and tender, but asked nothing. When the kiss ended, she felt lost and bereft.

He twined his fingers through her hair, staring at her so intently, he seemed to be memorizing her every feature. In barely more than a whisper he said, "I'll be back, darling. On the first day of spring. Watch for me."

He had almost reached the door when she found her voice. "Don't come back, Adam. Not in the spring. Not ever. Find someone who can walk in the sunlight with you."

"I have found her." He hadn't turned. Tracy could only see the strong angle of his shoulders and the handsome shape of his neck and head. "I've walked with her on Shadow. Someday she'll be ready to walk with me into the sun. And in the spring I'll come for her."

The sound of his car had long since faded before Tracy

turned from the door. In a trance she returned to her worktable and took up her tools again. For a long while she stared at the wood, then she lifted her knife and made the first cut. She knew now what this carving would be.

She worked steadily, without respite. To the observer there would have been no form or reason to the mis-shapen block, but in her torn heart and mind it had assumed the shape of a treasured memory.

As Tracy sat working in the solitude of her shop, a small car drew to a halt at the point where the road would take one last turn, blocking the valley from view. The man who sat behind the wheel stared up at Shadow.

"I'm leaving now," he said to the mountain. "But I'll be back. You've had her for years, but your time's over. Tracy doesn't know it yet, but she doesn't belong to you, just as she doesn't belong to me. Which of us will she choose?"

Slow minutes ticked away before he spoke again. "I'm going to beat you, Shadow. I'll be her choice. Not out of fear or emotional need, but because she loves me. By setting her free I can make her mine. Can you?"

He started his engine and released the brake. As he drove onto the pavement, he paused with one parting remark. "I'll be back for her in the spring."

Twice Bear looked in on Tracy, whimpered, then went away. As dusk began to fall he returned again. Padding over to her, he nudged her gently, a puzzled look in his eyes. His low worried whine finally penetrated her deep thought.

"Bear?" She looked up in surprise, finding that she had worked long past her usual time. "I see what you mean." She scratched him behind the ears. "It is too dark to work. Why don't we see what we have for supper that's quick and easy?"

She stood up, then looked down at the largest piece she had ever attempted. It would be hard, even likely to be beyond her skill. But it was a carving she had to do. She lovingly patted the shapeless mass, then, whistling for Bear, left the workshop.

Days flowed into weeks and then months. Tracy worked constantly on the figures of her carving. She cried her loneliest tears the day she knew there would be no child, that she had nothing left of Adam.

For the first time in her life she found the mountain lacking. With Bear close on her heels she wandered the roughest trails to return physically exhausted, but never at peace.

The people of the valley seldom saw her and when they did, each expressed shock at her look of fatigue. Tracy only shrugged away their concern and muttered that she was working very hard.

In the mail there was an occasional letter from Liza or a drawing from Summer. From Adam there was nothing. Since the day he had walked out of her workshop, he had virtually vanished from her life, but never from her thoughts.

Jed, good friend that he was, became her only link with Adam. Though he could barely afford it, he flew to New York City twice each month to see Liza. When he returned, Tracy battered him with questions almost faster than he could answer them.

Was Adam all right? Yes.

Was he sure? Absolutely!

Was Adam working too hard? Yes.

Had Adam shaved his beard? Yes.

And the mustache? No.

Did Adam ask about her? Yes.

*   *   *

Christmas came and went. There was a scarf from Summer but nothing from Adam. Summer's card of thanks only casually said that Daddy had liked Alice's flower. There was no word from Adam.

January was a dreadfully cold month. Tracy moved her carving into the house for the sake of conserving fuel. Consequently she worked even longer hours. During her frequent sleepless nights she found herself picking up her carving tools and beginning again on the wood.

Bear was her constant companion. She spoke to him of Adam. Her tears fell on his fur when she held him, wishing for someone to hold her. He became her link with reality, always there to remind her when it was time to eat or time to rest. He was the friend that Wolfe had been.

On the first day of February she made her decision. Because the lines were down in the valley, she drove to the next town. Shivering in a public phone booth, she dialed the number of the gallery that had contacted her with regularity since they had sold her "A Vixen at Play."

"This is Tracy Walker," she said when the phone was answered. "I'd like to speak with Barry Carrington, please." She waited, then a man identified himself as Carrington and asked if he could help her.

"Your gallery has been asking me to arrange a showing of my work." She paused and took a long, deep breath. "I've decided to give my consent."

The voice at the other end demurred until, with a sudden surge of confidence, Tracy interrupted.

"Perhaps I should have introduced myself as Trace."

The voice immediately changed tone. Of course the gallery would be more than pleased to display her work. A pause to check the calendar. April?

"No. That's too late," Tracy said resolutely. "It must be before spring."

Impossible. There wasn't enough time to make the

arrangements. Publicity and promotional campaigns took time.

"No publicity," Tracy said. "Private invitation only, until after the opening . . . in March."

March! Impossible.

"Thank you for your time, Mr. Carrington. Perhaps another gallery—"

The voice hastily capitulated. The show would be by private invitation and would open on March seventeenth. Would Trace be present?

"Yes."

Would any of the works be for immediate sale?

"Yes."

The call ended with the arrangements complete, and profuse apologies for not recognizing her at first.

Tracy had six busy weeks ahead of her. But with Jed's help she could do it.

"For heaven's sake, Adam. Stop fidgeting. It can't hurt you to wear that tuxedo for a few hours." Liza paced to the window, looked out, then paced back to the chair where Adam sat.

"Why should he want me to come to dinner with you, and why wear this stupid monkey suit?" Adam asked irritably.

"More like a penguin, I'd say," Liza said as she tried to stifle a smile.

The doorbell silenced any reply Adam might have made. Liza fairly flew to answer it. When she opened it Jed was waiting there, smiling and impressive in a tuxedo of his own. After a long, loving kiss for Liza, he greeted Adam.

"After that kiss," Adam said, "why would the two of you want me along as excess baggage?" He began to loosen his tie. "I think I'll stay home with a good book."

"No!" Jed and Liza said in unison.

"What on earth is wrong with the two of you? You're

both acting like you're walking on eggshells. If my not going makes you so nervous, then I'll go."

They were halfway across town before Adam showed any great curiosity about their destination. "What restaurants are in this part of town? I'm not familiar with any."

"Jed has another stop to make first." Liza looked worriedly at Jed for support.

"Yes. A friend of mine asked me to stop by the Carrington Gallery and look at a painting for him."

Adam was puzzled about which friend of Jed's had a penchant for art, but he asked no more questions. When the car was parked and Jed had helped Liza out of the car, Adam suggested that he wait for them there.

"No," Jed and Liza said again in unison.

"Are the two of you practicing to become a chorus?"

"No," Jed said. "But we'd both like your opinion on this work. It won't take but a minute."

Most ungraciously Adam consented and joined them on the sidewalk. The moment they entered the door he stopped in shock. When he turned to Jed and Liza they had mysteriously disappeared. The room was filled with elegantly dressed men and women, but it wasn't the people who interested Adam.

On tables draped with green velvet, on stands of walnut, on blocks of glass, and even on rough stone were graceful and lifelike carvings, each bearing the name Trace. Sarah's hummingbird was there and Ezra's dog. Jed's mallard shared a spot with a majestic eagle. A blue butterfly like Summer's rested on a delicate rose, and the chipmunk still slept curled on his leaf.

Adam's heart began to pound as he understood the meaning of this display. Urgently he searched the crowd for her . . . and she was there.

Dressed in a simple gray dress with her long hair coiled at the nape of her neck, she was the picture of composure. Her back was to him and she was chatting in a most relaxed way with a man who obviously appreciated her looks as well as her talent. A swift unreasonable jealousy surged through Adam, then she moved and he saw the carving.

"Tracy." He whispered her name as he absorbed the full impact of her work. There, captured in wood and painted with a breathtaking realism, were two people. A woman reclined on the mossy ground, clad only in a piece of sheer silk tied low over her hips. Her dark hair hid one breast. The man who bent over her and caressed her had hair of silver and the first beginnings of a dark beard. It bore the title "The Promise of Shadow, a Gift of Sunlight."

The card beneath the title stated in a bold black script that the carving was the property of Adam Grayson and not for sale. Adam was hardly aware of the crowd that moved about him. He was frozen, unable to move, until Tracy half turned and blocked the carving from view. Then he began to wend his way through the crowd.

Snatches of conversation floated about him, though nothing but Tracy penetrated his thoughts.

"Did you see that precious 'possum hanging by his tail?"

"The kitten tangled in a ball of yarn was my favorite."

"Her sketches are almost as breathtaking."

"I liked the skunk with the pink ribbon around his neck."

"Have you noticed that only one carving is of people."

"I asked James to buy that one for me, but it's most emphatically *not* for sale."

"My daughter lost her dog last week. She'll like the little beagle."

"I don't care how much you've been offered, Mr. Carrington. 'Sunlight' isn't mine to sell."

"Darling."

Tracy turned slowly toward him. Her eyes misted with a happy radiance

"Adam." His name on her lips was a healing balm for the aching loneliness of past months. Her gaze moved slowly over him. As if to assure herself that he was true and not her constant dream, she touched him. Her trembling fingers moved lightly over his clean-shaven jaw, barely brushing the edge of his mustache, and lingered for a fleeting second beneath his lips before falling away.

Adam could only look at her. She was thinner; there were dark smudges beneath her eyes from lack of sleep, but she was nonetheless lovely. He saw the glow that flushed her face and the light in her eyes, and knew it was meant for him. Yet none of the pretty speeches he had rehearsed would come.

"You never played your guitar for me," he said. It was a nonsensical thought that had appeared from nowhere.

"I know." Her husky voice was little more than a quiet whisper in the static air about them. "But I will, Adam. Anytime, and anywhere."

"Oh, love. Come here." With a rasping, shuddering groan, he drew her into his arms, forgetting the crowd around them. At this moment there was only Tracy, who with two words had given herself to him.

Anywhere and anytime. With these words she had made his life complete.

"Damn!" he muttered. "How long do you have to stay here?"

"Not one minute longer than you do."

"But your carvings? You wouldn't leave them."

"I would, for you."

"Tracy?"

"They don't matter like they did. I could never be careless about them, or callous, but nothing really matters but you."

"And Shadow?"

"She's a lovely mountain and I'd like to go back, but only with you, and only to visit."

"You're sure?" Nothing about him moved as he waited for her answer.

"Positive. My world is where you are."

"How would you like to go back to Shadow tonight?"

"Could we?"

"My bags have been packed for three days."

"But it's not the first of spring."

"How well I know. I don't think I would've made it."

"I've missed you, Adam."

"Don't look at me like that, Tracy, or we won't make it to Shadow." He took her arm and started walking to the exit.

"But how else can I look at you?"

"Oh, hell. Let's get out of here. By the way, how many bridesmaids do you want?"

"Well, let's see." She paused and thought. "There's Sarah, and Hester and Opal, and Liza, and Summer, and . . ."

"On second thought, maybe we'd better just elope."

"Sounds great to me."

"What?" Adam stopped abruptly in front of the door.

"I said to elope would be perfectly all right with me."

"Tracy, do you mean that?"

"I want *you*, Adam, not a fancy wedding."

"Then we'd better hurry. We have a detour to make on our way back to Shadow."

"Summer?"

"She's spending a few days with Marjorie." He laughed as a subtle hand began to show. "Guess who arranged it?"

"Liza?"

"Devious, isn't she?"

"Yes. Bless her."

Among the astonished crowd two people looked at each other and smiled as Adam and Tracy vanished through the exit. No one seemed to notice when the tall dark man dried tears from the cheeks of his red-haired companion and kissed the finger of her left hand that wore a sparkling diamond.

* * *

As moonlight filtered through the trees, casting patterns on the walls of the cabin, Adam stirred sleepily and drew Tracy to him. His hand wandered down her body to the slight swell of her abdomen.

"Are you sure?"

"Positive."

"How long?"

"Six weeks."

"Our first night back to Shadow."

"So it would seem."

"Will you be all right?"

"There's nothing to worry about."

"Darling, I . . ." Adam's breath caught in his throat. "Did you hear that?"

"Did I hear what, love?"

"It sounded like bagpipes."

Tracy laughed delightedly as she leaned over him. "At last you've heard the MacLaren's pipes."

"You've heard them?" he asked softly as he looked up at her.

"Yes."

"When?"

"The night I slept in your arms by Summer's bed."

"But you left me."

"I was frightened."

"And now?"

"Never again, Adam. Not as long as I have you."

"My last love, my true love."

"And mine," she whispered.

"Play, MacLaren, play." Adam drew her gently down to him.

Bear, who slept by the foot of their bed, hardly moved. He had in recent weeks grown accustomed to the strange behavior of his favorite humans. With a slight wag of his tail he settled back down to his dreams.

Far into the night Tracy slept in Adam's arms. Her dreams were of the silver-haired man who loved her; of

Summer who was sleeping contentedly nearby; and of the child who would be her Christmas gift for Adam.

Tomorrow this visit would end. But they would return, she, Adam, and their children. Someday she would tell them of Shadow, who had given her life and love.

EDITOR'S CORNER

Don't be surprised when you see our LOVESWEPT romances next month. No April Fool's joke . . . but we do hope to make you smile when you see our books on the racks. We've had a makeover! Our cover design has been revamped for our upcoming second year anniversary of the publication of LOVESWEPT. Ours is a svelte and lovely new look that doesn't just keep up with the times, but charges ahead of them. And the new colors are exquisite. We believe our new image is sophisticated and modern and we hope you enjoy it. Do let us know what you think.

We've other anniversary surprises in store for you . . . but not the least of them is some delightful romantic reading!

Warm and witty Billie Green leads off next month's LOVESWEPT list with her unforgettable love story, **DREAMS OF JOE,** LOVESWEPT #87. Imagine a famous hunk of a professional quarterback coming to live in a small town to coach the high school football team. Then add a beautiful young widow with two children . . . and a town full of the most warmhearted matchmakers. Now you have the delightful premise of **DREAMS OF JOE.** And for a long time, poor Abby thinks all she *will* be able to do with Joe is dream about him . . . because all those well-meaning folks who are throwing them at one another are also forever on hand! Oh, utter frustration! Oh, the resourcefulness needed to get a little privacy for some ordinary courtin'. We're sure you'll love every minute of Billie's high-spirited love story and that it will inspire a few dreams of your own.

Showing remarkable versatility, Joan Bramsch, noted

for her humor, has given us a heart-wrenchingly beautiful and sensual love story in **AT NIGHTFALL,** LOVESWEPT #88. Hero Matthew is a man with a handicap that is new to him, frightening, and cuts him off from all he loves best to do in the world. Then suddenly heroine Billy Theodore, a warm and honest woman, intrudes into his life . . . and lights it up! She adds a sense of fun and play to his existence while he frees her to know a new and delicious sensual awareness. But for both of them there seems a time on the horizon when they must part—especially when a miracle occurs! **AT NIGHTFALL** is a truly memorable romance.

We're very pleased to introduce you to the work of Anne and Ed Kolaczyk, a long and happily married couple, whose writing you've enjoyed in other romance lines and mainstream novels as well. But before they've always published under pen names. You'll read all about how they came to write together in their biographical sketch next month, but now let me hurry to a description of their charming debut book for us. **CAPTAIN WONDER,** LOVESWEPT #89, features a hero who *is* a hero! Mike Taylor is an actor who has achieved vast fame as television's Captain Wonder. Fleeing a mob of fans, he is befriended by heroine Sara Delaney's twin daughters. Those little girls are just as wild for the muscular marvel as others, even insisting their mom wear a Captain Wonder nightshirt, yet they are soothed in his presence. Not so Mom! Mike has a most unsettling effect on her. And, as circumstances draw them together on a trek that ends at Mike's California home, they find their attraction to one another irresistible! But, there's a key question: can an ordinary smalltown woman face up to a life in the fast lane with a famous television star? The answer is heartwarming in this love story you won't want to miss!

Joan Elliott Pickart is becoming a regular on the LOVESWEPT list, as well as a real favorite! No where is her talent in creating riveting romances more evident than in her offering next month, **LOOK FOR THE SEA GULLS,** LOVESWEPT #90. Record temperatures prevail when Tracey Tate arrives in Texas to write a story on Matt Ramsey's Rocking R ranch. Immediately, too, the temperature soars within his air-conditioned house as these two fiery personalities clash . . . and learn to love. But like his father, Matt cherishes his land which he has always put ahead of everything else in life. And Tracey finds herself to be a very possessive woman where her heart is concerned. How these two sensual, emotional people resolve their conflicts makes for the very best in romance reading!

We hope you'll agree with those of us who work on the LOVESWEPT line that we've provided you with four equally wonderful romances next month. And of course we're sure you won't miss any of them—even with that high-fashion new look on our covers!

Sincerely,

Carolyn Nichols

Carolyn Nichols
  Editor
LOVESWEPT
Bantam Books, Inc.
666 Fifth Avenue
New York, NY 10103

Dear Loveswept Readers,

On the pages that follow you will find an excerpt from my new Bantam novel, PROMISES & LIES. Publication of this is an exciting event for me, and I thought I'd share with you a little of the story and how I came to write it.

I think the development of a person is fascinating, like taking a blank canvas and watching design and color create form. I wanted to do this with a young woman, and Valerie Cardell, the heroine of PROMISES & LIES, became this young woman. Three men at different stages of her life influence and help shape the woman she becomes because I believe that without romance and love, no woman's development is ever complete! I also have long been fascinated by sibling rivalry, especially between sisters, and in PROMISES & LIES, Valerie's road to happiness is often made rocky and treacherous as a result of her sister.

I set out to write a modern-day Cinderella story because I still believe in fairy tales, especially one with love, romance, danger—and of course, a happy ending. Like you and me, the heroine of this novel has her fantasies, and the fun of writing the story was that I could make sure all her dreams came true!

Happy Reading!

Susanne Jaffe

Susanne Jaffe

They drove in silence, Valerie pretending to herself that she did not know what was about to happen. He was taking her to his apartment and he was going to make love to her. That's what she wanted too, wasn't it? He would kiss her, whisper encouraging love words to her, and touch her and touch her and touch her until her skin was on fire. He would find out she was a virgin. She had to tell him. Would that turn him off? No, he would be proud that she was giving him such a special gift. And he would be gentle with her. But he might also be disappointed and she could not bear the thought of that.

Valerie had gone out with Teddy for more than three months, and had considered getting married, but had not been able to have sex with him. She had known Roger Monash for less than two weeks and she was worrying about not being able to please him in bed. She never questioned her feelings for him or what the outcome of this intimacy would be. Irrational, illogical, uncharacteristically impetuous as it might be, Valerie knew she loved him. She could not conceive of his feeling differently. The very intensity of her emotion bespoke its rightness. She did not think she was being naïve, only truer to herself than she had ever been before. And she was too innocent and inexperienced to understand the vast difference between longing and loving. She had no qualms, therefore, about doing the right thing, only about doing it right.

"Is this where you live?" she asked tremulously as they climbed the stairs of a small apartment building near downtown Dallas.

"Uh, no, this belongs to a friend of mine."

"Why can't we go to your place?"

"I loaned it out to a buddy. I wasn't sure you and I would be using it, and besides, he's married, so if I can help the poor sucker out, why not?"

Valerie nodded her understanding, but her stomach gave a funny little lurch.

"Roger, maybe we should wait," she said when they entered the apartment. It was a dismal place, with a hodgepodge of dusty furniture and a view of a parking lot. "I'm sure your place is much nicer and—"

"Who gives a shit about nice. All I care about is that I want you." He crushed her against him and kissed her deeply. "Now tell me," he whispered against her ear, "do you really want to wait?"

She shook her head and smiled up at him, eyes glistening with love. "Roger," she said softly, stepping slightly out of the circle of his arms. "I'm a virgin."

His laugh was a crude, harsh snort that Valerie pretended not to hear. "Sure. And I'm Santa Claus. Come on, get serious. If there was ever a stew who was a virgin she'd be kicked out for poor job performance."

"It's true," she said, ignoring the quick stab of hurt.

He looked hard at her. "You're telling me the truth, aren't you?" She nodded. "Why me?"

She tilted her head, surprise evident on her face. "Because I love you."

Roger Monash did not answer immediately, but a frown flashed across his Kennedy-like face, as if he was considering just how much of a bastard he really was. What he saw as he looked at Valerie was a lovely young face filled with trust, and a body that had been tormenting his dreams for a week. She had to lose it sometime, he thought selfishly, it might as well be to him.

"I love you too, baby," he said as he took her back in his arms. "And I won't hurt you. I promise."

"Could I have a drink?"

"Sure."

She followed him into a sliver of kitchen and watched him fumble around looking for the liquor and glasses. Without asking what she wanted, he poured her a glass of Scotch, neat, and she gulped it down, grateful for its warmth. She was beginning to feel chilled, as if only now the cold reality of the situation was dawning on her.

Then she was being led into a bedroom, and Roger was kissing her, his tongue prying her lips apart, his hands roaming over her back, to her shoulders, down to her hips. "Val, oh, Val, you feel so good, baby," he murmured against her ear. His hands were on the cool skin of her back as he pushed up her sweater; then he was unhooking her bra, lifting it away. He lowered his head, and his tongue caressed first one nipple, then the other, his breath scorching her as much as his touch.

"Take off your clothes. I can't stand this another minute."

"Roger, maybe—"

"I said get undressed." He turned away and took off his clothes, unaware that Valerie had not moved. She tried to unbutton her skirt, but her fingers were trembling so badly that she could not grip the button. Her sweater and bra were still bunched up over her breasts, her hands dangling by her sides. She felt miserable, foolish, incapable of doing anything to help herself.

When Roger was naked, he faced her. Whatever embarrassment and awkwardness she might have experienced during her first encounter with a naked man was mitigated by her awe at his physical beauty. His muscles rippled like those of a thoroughbred stallion. Shoulders, chest, tapering waist; lean, firm thighs: this was a body of power, a body almost audacious in its perfection. Her eyes followed the mat of sandy hair on his chest to its thinning trail, then darted up again to meet the grin on his face.

"Come on, honey, don't be shy," he said softly. "I'll help you."

Seconds later she was naked, on her back, willing herself to feel the warmth that Roger's kisses and touch usually inspired in her. But she felt oddly dispassionate as he murmured in her ear, kissed her neck and breasts and nipples and stomach, touched her in secret places and sacred places. Was it fear that had taken control, or was it something deeper, more vital? Thoughts suddenly fled as she felt him throbbing against her thigh, and then he hoisted himself above her.

"It'll hurt for a second and then it'll be fine," he assured her, and she kept her eyes wide open, nodded, wishing it was over, wishing more that she would feel something, even the pain.

*   *   *

It was from three this morning until five that Valerie had permitted herself to dwell on what she had done. Until then, she had found things to occupy her thoughts, to keep her from remembering how pleasureless Saturday night had been, and how a repetition of the sex Sunday afternoon and evening had left her similarly unmoved. She told herself that it was her fault; she was inexperienced and therefore scared, inhibited, inept, inadequate. She still loved Roger, she told herself; he had been kind and thoughtful each time. If it bothered her that Sunday they had gone straight to his friend's apartment and had stayed there all day, she let herself be convinced that Roger's needs were more urgent than her own, and that once the newness became part of a practiced routine, they would do things together, things that had nothing to do with sex. She told herself that he would never grow bored with her as he had with Wanda Eberle. She told herself that she had not been used.

In those two hours when night was at its

unfriendliest and morning seemed a light at the end of an infinite tunnel, when time turned threatening and thoughts turned to unavoidable truths, Valerie was thankful that Linda was sleeping. Whatever she was telling herself, she knew she would not be able to say it to Linda with any conviction. But now, as they walked together silently to get their uniforms, she had a feeling that the confrontation was imminent.

"Should I start or will you?" Linda asked quietly, keeping her eyes straight ahead.

"I suppose it will have to be you because I have nothing to say." Valerie despised herself for acting this way. She did not resent her friend's prying because she knew it came from caring. She was scared of Linda—scared to hear her speak with knowledge that Valerie would refute without sincerity.

Linda stopped and reached out to hold Valerie back from walking ahead. The two girls faced each other, Valerie's expression challenging and proud. Linda's eyes shone with anger.

"You went to bed with him, didn't you?"

"Who?"

"Who! How many could there be?"

"If you mean Roger, the answer is yes."

Linda shook her head in amazement. "Didn't I warn you? Didn't I tell you what he did to Wanda? How could you be so stupid, Val? How?"

"If you think it's stupid for two people in love to do what comes naturally, that's your problem, and I'm sincerely sorry for you," she said haughtily.

"In love! You're an even bigger fool than I thought," Linda yelled.

"I don't have to listen to this!" Valerie started to walk away, but Linda's hand was on her arm.

"Do you really think he's in love with you? Be honest, do you?"

"He said so and I believe him."

" 'He said so and I believe him.' You're incredible, you really are."

"I would appreciate your not repeating everything I say. And I suggest that we save this little chat for another time. We're going to be late."

"We have plenty of time, and besides, this won't wait. You've been deliberately avoiding me since Saturday and I—"

"I haven't noticed you trying to be with me, either," Valerie cut in.

"Of course not, you idiot. What did you want me to do, rush up and ask for a blow-by-blow description! I figured that you would *want* to talk with me—that what happened to you was important and you would want to share it with a friend. Obviously, you're so ashamed you can't even face me. That's why I knew I had to bring it up first."

"I am *not* ashamed!" Valerie retorted hotly. "What Roger and I did was beautiful and special. We're in love with each other. Why won't you believe me?"

Linda took a deep breath, briefly shut her eyes, and said: "I do believe you, Val. I believe that you love him and that you think he loves you. But let me just ask a few questions, okay?"

Valerie nodded, dreading what was coming.

"Did he take you to a friend's apartment, saying his was too far or that he had loaned it to a married friend? Did he tell you that he couldn't fly for wanting you so badly? Did he take you to bed Sunday and stay there with you all day? Did he say he can't make plans for when he'll see you next, it depends on his schedule? Did he—"

"Stop it, stop it!" Valerie shrieked, covering her ears with her hands. Gently, Linda lowered them and took Valerie in her arms. Soundlessly, Valerie sobbed, for being a fool and a coward.

"I'm sorry," Linda said softly. "I didn't want to have to hurt you this way, but I didn't know what else to do. You had to see what was going on, what kind of bastard you were getting involved with."

"How did you know he said those things to me? How did you know about his friend's apartment?"

"The answer to the first question is easy. He used the same lines on both me and Wanda. As for the second, while you've been out of it these past few days, I asked around a little. It seems that Mr. Swinging Singles Monash shares an apartment with three other guys, two to a bedroom. When he's in Dallas, he hits on anyone he knows who has a place to himself."

For a moment Valerie said nothing, staring at her roommate but seeing beyond her to the dingy, dreary, unkempt apartment with its parking-lot view. "What am I going to do?" she whispered.

"What do you want to do?"

"I *don't* want to go to bed with him again."

"Not good, huh?"

"Well, I'm sure it's my fault, but no, not too good."

"Why do you think it was your fault?"

"I'm not very experienced, after all, so I probably don't know what I'm doing."

"Your pleasure comes from *his* knowing what to do, kiddo, not you."

"Well, still, I think I'll save sex for another time."

"Another man, Val, not another time. Roger Monash simply was not the right man. Not for someone like you."

"Why *not* someone like me?" Valerie demanded, tired of being different, of being unable to do what other grown women did. What made her so special? What made her so unable to pretend?

"Because your innocence won't disappear no matter how many men you have, even if they're all like Roger Monash," Linda said with a small smile. "You deserve someone who can appreciate that innocence. I'm not saying he has to love you, Val, but there are men who will recognize your purity and admire it. If you want to experiment with sex, do it with them, not with selfish bastards like Monash."

Valerie thought about what Linda said. "You're not like that, are you?" she asked gently. Linda shook her head. "Why not? What makes me this way, and why am I so embarrassed by it?"

"Oh, Val, don't ask me questions like that. I'm not smart enough to answer them."

"You're smarter than I'll ever be," Valerie said miserably.

"No, just not as nice."

The girls looked at each other and broke into laughter, but for Valerie the sound was bittersweet. She would be seeing Roger the next night and she did not know how to tell him there would be no sex. She had a feeling that telling him she did not love him would not matter as much to him.

#1 HEAVEN'S PRICE
By Sandra Brown
Blair Simpson had enclosed herself in the fortress of her dancing, but Sean Garrett was determined to love her anyway. In his arms she came to understand the emotions behind her dancing. But could she afford the high price of love?

#2 SURRENDER
By Helen Mittermeyer
Derry had been pirated from the church by her ex-husband, from under the nose of the man she was to marry. She remembered every detail that had driven them apart—and the passion that had drawn her to him. The unresolved problems between them grew . . . but their desire swept them toward surrender.

#3 THE JOINING STONE
By Noelle Berry McCue
Anger and desire warred within her, but Tara Burns was determined not to let Damon Mallory know her feelings. When he'd walked out of their marriage, she'd been hurt.

Damon had violated a sacred trust, yet her passion for him was as breathtaking as the Grand Canyon.

#4 SILVER MIRACLES
By Fayrene Preston
Silver-haired Chase Colfax stood in the Texas moonlight, then took Trinity Ann Warrenton into his arms. Overcome by her own needs, yet determined to have him on her own terms, she struggled to keep from losing herself in his passion.

#5 MATCHING WITS
By Carla Neggers
From the moment they met, Ryan Davis tried to outmaneuver Abigail Lawrence. She'd met her match in the Back Bay businessman. And Ryan knew the Boston lawyer was more woman than any he'd ever encountered. Only if they vanquished their need to best the other could their love triumph.

#6 A LOVE FOR ALL TIME
By Dorothy Garlock
A car crash had left its marks on Casey Farrow's beauty. So what were Dan

Murdock's motives for pursuing her? Guilt? Pity? Casey had to choose. She could live with doubt and fear . . . or learn a lesson in love.

#7 A TRYST WITH MR. LINCOLN?
By Billie Green
When Jiggs O'Malley awakened in a strange hotel room, all she saw were the laughing eyes of stranger Matt Brady . . . all she heard were his teasing taunts about their "night together" . . . and all she remembered was nothing! They evaded the passions that intoxicated them until . . . there was nowhere to flee but into each other's arms.

#8 TEMPTATION'S STING
By Helen Conrad
Taylor Winfield likened Rachel Davidson to a Conus shell, contradictory and impenetrable. Rachel battled for independence, torn by her need for Taylor's embraces and her impassioned desire to be her own woman. Could they both succumb to the temptation of the tropi-

cal paradise and still be true to their hearts?

#9 DECEMBER 32nd . . . AND ALWAYS
By Marie Michael
Blaise Hamilton made her feel like the most desirable woman on earth. Pat opened herself to emotions she'd thought buried with her late husband. Together they were unbeatable as they worked to build the jet of her late husband's dreams. Time seemed to be running out and yet—would ALWAYS be long enough?

#10 HARD DRIVIN' MAN
By Nancy Carlson
Sabrina sensed Jacy in hot pursuit, as she maneuvered her truck around the racetrack, and recalled his arms clasping her to him. Was he only using her feelings so he could take over her trucking company? Their passion knew no limits as they raced full speed toward love.

#11 BELOVED INTRUDER
By Noelle Berry McCue
Shannon Douglas hated

Michael Brady from the moment he brought the breezes of life into her shadowy existence. Yet a specter of the past remained to torment her and threaten their future. Could he subdue the demons that haunted her, and carry her to true happiness?

#12 HUNTER'S PAYNE
By Joan J. Domning
P. Lee Payne strode into Karen Hunter's office demanding to know why she was stalking him. She was determined to interview the mysterious photographer. She uncovered his concealed emotions, but could the secrets their hearts confided protect their love, or would harsh daylight shatter their fragile alliance?

#13 TIGER LADY
By Joan J. Domning
Who *was* this mysterious lover she'd never seen who courted her on the office computer, and nicknamed her Tiger Lady? And could he compete with Larry Hart, who came to repair the computer and stayed to short-circuit her emotions? How could she choose between poetry and passion—between soul and Hart?

#14 STORMY VOWS
By Iris Johansen
Independent Brenna Sloan wasn't strong enough to reach out for the love she needed, and Michael Donovan knew only how to take—until he met Brenna. Only after a misunderstanding nearly destroyed their happiness, did they surrender to their fiery passion.

#15 BRIEF DELIGHT
By Helen Mittermeyer
Darius Chadwick felt his chest tighten with desire as Cygnet Melton glided into his life. But a prelude was all they knew before Cyg fled in despair, certain she had shattered the dream they had made together. Their hearts had collided in an instant; now could they seize the joy of enduring love?

#16 A VERY RELUCTANT KNIGHT
By Billie Green
A tornado brought them together in a storm cel-

lar. But Maggie Sims and Mark Wilding were anything but perfectly matched. Maggie wanted to prove he was wrong about her. She knew they didn't belong together, but when he caressed her, she was swept up in a passion that promised a lifetime of love.

#17 TEMPEST AT SEA
By Iris Johansen
Jane Smith sneaked aboard playboy-director Jake Dominic's yacht on a dare. The muscled arms that captured her were inescapable—and suddenly Jane found herself agreeing to a month-long cruise of the Caribbean. Jane had never given much thought to love, but under Jake's tutelage she discovered its magic . . . and its torment.

#18 AUTUMN FLAMES
By Sara Orwig
Lily Dunbar had ventured too far into the wilderness of Reece Wakefield's vast Chilean ranch; now an oncoming storm thrust her into his arms . . . and he refused to let her go. Could he lure her, step by seductive step, away from the life she had forged for herself, to find her real home in his arms?

#19 PFARR LAKE AFFAIR
By Joan J. Domning
Leslie Pfarr hadn't been back at her father's resort for an hour before she was pitched into the lake by Eric Nordstrom! The brash teenager who'd made her childhood a constant torment had grown into a handsome man. But when he began persuading her to fall in love, Leslie wondered if she was courting disaster.

#20 HEART ON A STRING
By Carla Neggers
One look at heart surgeon Paul Houghton Welling told JoAnna Radcliff he belonged in the stuffy society world she'd escaped for a cottage in Pigeon Cove. She firmly believed she'd never fit into his life, but he set out to show her she was wrong. She was the puppet master, but he knew how to keep her heart on a string.

#21 THE SEDUCTION OF JASON

By Fayrene Preston

On vacation in Martinique, Morgan Saunders found Jason Falco. When a misunderstanding drove him away, she had to win him back. She played the seductress to tempt him to return; she sent him tropical flowers to tantalize him; she wrote her love in letters twenty feet high—on a billboard that echoed the words in her heart.

#22 BREAKFAST IN BED

By Sandra Brown

For all Sloan Fairchild knew, Hollywood had moved to San Francisco when mystery writer Carter Madison stepped into her bed-and-breakfast inn. In his arms the forbidden longing that throbbed between them erupted. Sloan had to choose—between her love for him and her loyalty to a friend . . .

#23 TAKING SAVANNAH

By Becky Combs

The Mercedes was headed straight for her! Cassie hurled a rock that smashed the antique car's taillight. The price driver Jake Kilrain exacted was a passionate kiss, and he set out to woo the Southern lady, Cassie, but discovered that his efforts to conquer the lady might end in his own surrender . . .

#24 THE RELUCTANT LARK

By Iris Johansen

Her haunting voice had earned Sheena Reardon fame as Ireland's mournful dove. Yet to Rand Challon the young singer was not just a lark but a woman whom he desired with all his heart. Rand knew he could teach her to spread her wings and fly free, but would her flight take her from him or into his arms forever?

#25 LIGHTNING THAT LINGERS

By Sharon and Tom Curtis

He was the Cougar Club's star attraction, mesmerizing hundreds of women with hips that swayed in the provocative motions of love. Jennifer Hamilton offered her heart to the kindred spirit, the tender poet in him. But Philip's worldly side was alien to her, threatening to unravel the magical threads binding them . . .

#26 ONCE IN A BLUE MOON
By Billie Green

Arlie was reckless, wild, a little naughty—but in the nicest way! Whenever she got into a scrape, Dan was always there to rescue her. But this time Arlie wanted a very *personal* bailout that only *he* could provide. Dan never could say no to her. After all, the special favor she wanted was his own secret wish—wasn't it?

#27 THE BRONZED HAWK
By Iris Johansen

Kelly would get her story even if it meant using a bit of blackmail. She'd try anything to get inventor-genius Nick O'Brien to take her along in his experimental balloon. Nick had always trusted his fate to the four winds and the seven seas . . . until a feisty lady clipped his wings by losing herself in his arms . . .

#28 LOVE, CATCH A WILD BIRD
By Anne Reisser

Daredevil and dreamer, Bree Graeme collided with Cane Taylor on her family's farm—and there was an instant intimacy between them. Bree's wild years came to a halt, for when she looked into Cane's eyes, she knew she'd found love at last. But what price freedom to dare when the man she loved could rest only as she lay safe in his arms?

#29 THE LADY AND THE UNICORN
By Iris Johansen

Janna Cannon scaled the walls of Rafe Santine's estate, determined to appeal to the man who could save her animal preserve. She bewitched his guard dogs, then cast a spell over him as well. She offered him a gift he'd never dared risk reaching for before—but could he trust his emotions enough to open himself to her love?

 # LOVESWEPT

Love Stories you'll never forget
by authors you'll always remember

☐	21603	**Heaven's Price** #1 Sandra Brown	$1.95
☐	21604	**Surrender** #2 Helen Mittermeyer	$1.95
☐	21600	**The Joining Stone** #3 Noelle Berry McCue	$1.95
☐	21601	**Silver Miracles** #4 Fayrene Preston	$1.95
☐	21605	**Matching Wits** #5 Carla Neggers	$1.95
☐	21606	**A Love for All Time** #6 Dorothy Garlock	$1.95
☐	21609	**Hard Drivin' Man** #10 Nancy Carlson	$1.95
☐	21610	**Beloved Intruder** #11 Noelle Berry McCue	$1.95
☐	21611	**Hunter's Payne** #12 Joan J. Domning	$1.95
☐	21618	**Tiger Lady** #13 Joan Domning	$1.95
☐	21613	**Stormy Vows** #14 Iris Johansen	$1.95
☐	21614	**Brief Delight** #15 Helen Mittermeyer	$1.95
☐	21616	**A Very Reluctant Knight** #16 Billie Green	$1.95
☐	21617	**Tempest at Sea** #17 Iris Johansen	$1.95
☐	21619	**Autumn Flames** #18 Sara Orwig	$1.95
☐	21620	**Pfarr Lake Affair** #19 Joan Domning	$1.95
☐	21621	**Heart on a String** #20 Carla Neggars	$1.95
☐	21622	**The Seduction of Jason** #21 Fayrene Preston	$1.95
☐	21623	**Breakfast In Bed** #22 Sandra Brown	$1.95
☐	21624	**Taking Savannah** #23 Becky Combs	$1.95
☐	21625	**The Reluctant Lark** #24 Iris Johansen	$1.95

Prices and availability subject to change without notice.

Buy them at your local bookstore or use this handy coupon for ordering:

Bantam Books, Inc., Dept. SW, 414 East Golf Road, Des Plaines, Ill. 60016

Please send me the books I have checked above. I am enclosing
$_____ (please add $1.25 to cover postage and handling). Send
check or money order—no cash or C.O.D.'s please.

Mr/Ms _____

Address _____

City/State _____ Zip _____

SW—3/85

Please allow four to six weeks for delivery. This offer expires 9/85.

LOVESWEPT

Love Stories you'll never forget
by authors you'll always remember